THE FLIGHT OF THE
STONEMAN'S SON

Book 1 The Stoneman Series

Terence Munsey

Munsey Music
Toronto Los Angeles London

This book is entirely a work of fiction. Any resemblance to actual people, places, events, names, incidences, living or dead, is totally coincidental. This work is entirely the product of the author's imagination.

THE FLIGHT OF THE STONEMAN'S SON

published by:

Munsey Music

Box 511, Richmond Hill, Ontario, Canada, L4C 4Y8

Fax: 905 737 0208

Canadian Cataloguing in Publication Data

Munsey, Terence, 1953-
    The Flight of the stoneman's son
(The stoneman series ; bk. 1)
ISBN 0-9697066-0-X

I. Title. II. Series: Munsey, Terence, 1953-
The stoneman series ; bk. 1

PS8576.U5753F56 1994   C813'.54   C94-932763-8
PR9199.3.M85F56 1994

Library of Congress Catalogue Number 93-93660

First Munsey Music original soft cover printing: April 1993
Second soft cover printing: 1995

Cover design, back note and illustration art © 1993 by Terence Munsey

Manufactured in Canada

Acknowledgments

To: Basil, Tere, Margherita, Christina, Jack, Lynn, Simon, Daniel, Juliana, Carol-Lynn, Willi, Melissa, Alice, Nicolas, Samantha, Fred, Stanford University, and Lady 'D' for all the support and inspiration that eventually found its way into the creation of this story.

To Wendy Silverberg for spending the time proof reading and editing the final manuscript. Thank you. It will always be greatly appreciated.

To Christina Beaumont for proof reading the laser 'camera ready' document and her editorial suggestions on the first printing, and then for re-proofing the second printing 'camera ready' document.

To Stewart and Evelyn for helping to answer some of my many questions.

<u>Books by Terence Munsey in
The Stoneman Series:</u>

THE FLIGHT OF THE STONEMAN'S SON

ISBN 0-9697066-0-X

LCCN 93-93660

Book 1

THE KEEPER OF THREE

ISBN 0-9697066-1-8

LCCN 93-86550

Book 2

LABYRINTHS OF LIGHT

ISBN 0-9697066-2-6

LCCN 95-94007

Book 3

MARKS OF STONE

ISBN 0-9697066-3-4

Book 4

Available at your bookstore

Thank you for coming as far as you could.
The pathways are richer.

Chapter 1.

This is the beginning of a wondrous adventure and I am to take you there. Where should I begin? At this moment I am back here, safely sitting in front of the large stone fireplace built by my father so long ago.

I remember helping cut and carry each stone. Watching and learning like a young apprentice, preparing for a long life and career. Hoping to acquire the craftsmanship; a craftsmanship that I might one day in my turn, pass on to my son. What a simple existence it all should have been. I find myself longing for the security of those times gone by and at the same instant pleased and proud of my part in this adventure! An adventure that once we are all comfortable, I will begin to tell.

Though the air is warmed by the safe yellowish red glow of the fire, the damp cool days of my story have not yet fully evaporated. They may never entirely leave. They have crystallized into a series of deep memories, with their dangers and triumphs lingering. As ghouls and phantoms they exist in the dark secret regions. They wait like chained dogs for their chance of escape, so that they can momentarily, in their sense of never ending time, terrorize and roam free again. They wait until another young stonemason's son is called by the powers beyond, or should I say chosen, no volunteered, to return them back to their own worlds. We will never be the same again!

There's nothing like a pipe to soothe one before a long accounting. Let me see...

It was a summer's late afternoon. The garden was billowing with the green of the shrubs and trees; the various colored flowers in their last display of excellence. There was a sense of calm, of nature at rest, yet, at the same time, a sense of an uneasiness. You know, like those days at the beginning of August that warn of the approaching changes of fall. It was a foreboding moment of peace.

My nephews were coming to visit and bring news on the preparations of the village for Summer Festival. The Festival was an annual occurrence dating well beyond memory, stretching to a long forgotten time where magic and kinship existed as commonplace as a simple greeting wave today.

This season was different. The young amongst the village seemed more bewitched than previous celebrations. There was something wrong. Everything was too perfect. I...

"Hi...Uncle Julian...Are you there?"

The first of my two visitors, Eruinn, began to appear on the path. He was big and towered over most of the other youngsters his own age as well as the majority of his elders! His face was round and his dark hair cropped short above smallish ears. This allowed his sensitive and welcoming visage to be quickly focused upon by any he encountered. He exuded a spirit that was controlled yet unpredictable. Most mistakenly thought that he was the eldest of my two nephews. He was of the gentlest, well meaning temperament. His feet were on the earth, his mind methodical and precise. If you asked him to do a task he would not rest till it was completed to perfection. As a result, he gave the impression that he was older than his brother, Thiunn, who was lagging behind on the path just looking for a chance to bait this larger, younger brother.

"Yeo...Uncle J...Are you here?" Thiunn was smiling. He was always cheery. Nothing ever seemed to cause him to think too long on the practical importants that kept Eruinn stolidly on his path.

Unlike Eruinn, Thiunn was noticeably more slender. He had the physique of the long distance runner. Though not weak, he was more physically fragile than his brother. As a result, he had focused upon developing his quick wittedness and come to rely, at this early age with his good looks and unkempt fair hair, upon his natural abilities to charm and influence those he met. He was self assured. This gave the impression of being mischievous. His spirit was young and refreshing. He intuitively knew he was in total control of his destiny, though he had no idea what it was! His life was set. Today would change all of this. Imagine how such an inconsequential visit should lead us all together to do things we never thought would ever be more than dreams or story land adventures.

"Hello there, you're early! I just buttered the bread and the tea is almost ready. Sit down. Tell me of the preparations."

Both sat. They began to talk, one cutting in just as the other finished. It was as if they were of one mind. Thinking back now, I should have been more aware of this phenomenon and the other strange coincidences of that afternoon tea.

"I had better check the kettle. Who would like jam and bread with their tea?"

Both nodded. I rose to get the kettle when, a loud clang sounded, stopping me in mid step. A cloaked figure was hurrying past the garden gate to the north side of the cottage and down the path toward us. We were all startled by the noise and sight of this stranger. We looked to one another without saying a word. Each of us silently wondering: 'who is this?'

"I'll have two sugar roots with mine, thank you." directed the figure as it approached the three of us. We were still spellbound by the sudden appearance of this intruder.

"Well, don't you remember me Julian?"

Suddenly, as if it were just two moments before, I knew. It was 'D', as she preferred to be called. I never

knew what the 'D' stood for, just that she liked to be
addressed that way. The little I knew of her was that
she came from the mountain country to the Northeast,
and that she was alone in this world, as all her family
had been killed in the Separation War.

She was a striking rugged woman, muscular but pe-
tite. She carried herself with the proud stature of an
aristocrat. To some she was intimidating in her taut
beauty and keen thought. It was said she was a descen-
dent of the Old Ones and possessed great magic and
power.

We had met five summers ago about this time during
the Festival. I had bumped into her, causing her to fall
and drop the bag of crafts and medicinal herbs that she
would sell during the five days and nights of the
festivities. As I threw out my hand to help raise her
from the ground, our eyes caught for an instant and I
realized that this was a very old friend. But how? I was
certain we had never met before. At least, not in this
life. We introduced ourselves and chatted for a few
moments. Before we parted, I apologized and inquired
into her purpose and where she was staying while in
the village. Feeling responsible for her tumble, I
offered my hospitality if ever she was in need or just
on the pathway. That was it. Now, out of the blue 'D'
was here five years later for tea!

"Oh 'D'. Are you here again for the celebrations?
How are you? These are my nephews..."

As I turned to introduce them, I noticed a certain understanding familiarity between 'D' and these two
youngsters. Just as I had had, five years ago.

"No need to introduce me Julian. This is Eruinn and
Thiunn. I would have known them anywhere. Hello."
she put out her beautifully smooth yet strong hand to
greet them. As she leaned forward we each noticed
that she was hurt.

"Is something wrong?" she asked.

"Your tunic...it's ripped and..." I was about to say
bloody as she nonchalantly declared:

"Oh that, I caught myself on a briar in the woods. It's nothing. I will clean up after tea if you can provide me with a clean shirt and washing basin. Right now I am weary and exhausted from my travels. Let me rest awhile. This tea looks tremendous!"

"Certainly!" jumped in Eruinn, "Thiunn, go get the basin, and I'll find a shirt, if that's all right with you Uncle Julian? Then after tea it will all be ready and waiting."

"Uncle Julian?" questioned 'D'. "Don't you mean."…She stopped in mid sentence…"Never mind, we will get to that in due course."

The two youngsters stared at me, then at 'D' with surprise and questions in their glances. I looked to 'D' with the same inquisitiveness. Then the two quickly ran off to accomplish their tasks, returning in what seemed a few very short moments.

"It's all ready…whenever you want…inside the guest room," informed Thiunn, between breaths.

"Thank you young masters. Such service is reminiscent of the OLD TIMES. Please sit. I'll pour the tea once Julian stops that iron kettle and fills the pot. By the way," she turned to Julian, "Put some of these herbs in the pot. They will add flavor to the tea and rekindle the strength to us all. We will need it."

This was another strange occurrence I should have paid more attention to at the time, but the kettle was boiling over and the day was becoming late. Things pass without explanation when you have guests to feed and tend to. It was time for more tea.

After we had finished the tea and all the required polite conversation pleasantries, 'D' went into the cottage to clean up her tangle with the briar. When she was out of sight, Eruinn and Thiunn blurted out in unison:

"WOW! Where did you meet her? When? How? Why didn't you speak of this before?!"

I retold the story of the meeting five years before.

"Oh come on," commented Thiunn. "You can tell us the real truth! We're both almost grown ups now."

I assured them that they now knew as much as there ever was to know, but I could tell they still didn't quite believe. Both looked offended that 'Uncle Julian' hadn't treated them as his equals and totally confided in them, as they would now feel at ease to do with him, if there was anything to confide, that is.

Before I was able to continue with anything more, 'D' returned. She looked stunning with her silky hair and taut body. There was a knowing glint in her large eyes. Her stare penetrated the depths within. It momentarily paralyzed me. Quickly I averted her attracting eyes, noticing that her wound was taken care of and that she was wearing the red shirt Eruinn had laid out. There was a new item unnoticed before, being slightly covered by her cloak, a sword. Not just any sword, but a jeweled sparkling one. It looked very old but also brand new. 'D' stood, her legs shoulder width apart, her hands on her hips.

"Well," she bellowed, breaking our apparent trance. "I think it is now time to explain why I am here, and who you really are!"

Chapter 2.

Far to the barren northlands, deep within the earth, comes an unheard cry. The Gotts are busy. They are working their prisoner slaves day and night. Cruel torture is the reward given to any tired or sick under the direction of their whip! They are digging down with a frenzy not seen since the days of Ho.

Lord Ho was their exulted feared leader during the Separation War. The mere utterance of his name bred dread and panic through foe and friend alike. It was under his tutelage that the Gotts, not a very bright tribe, almost succeeded in the complete absorption of this third planet, our tranquil blue home.

Lord Ho had summoned the Magic of the Lake of Choices with his evil, only in the end to be destroyed by that same power. So why all the digging?

The Gotts had never been known for their kindness, but these past personal attributes had become forgotten through the years. The various northern bordering villages and tribes, in their effort to recapture the 'normalcy' of the time before Ho, were willing to appease and let well enough alone and forgotten.

For the poor unfortunate traveler lost on the paths of the Burning Forest or the mountain passes of Gott, there was no help or escape—just enslavement till death.

The Gotts were conniving and mean in attitude and looks. To differentiate male from female visually was impossible. Only through capture could the difference be easily discovered. The female was much more abusive and aggressive on slave victims than the male. This was probably due to the Gott females complete dominance by the male in all other aspects of Gott existence and tradition; except within the slave training arena where the female predominated and was allowed act as she wished. All their subservient anger and frustration was vented upon any newly captured slaves. This perversely amused and entertained the male Gott.

Along the lands to the North there had been many recent reports of missing travelers. These unfortunate souls now knew the female from male Gott. There were also newer dangers on the roadways of strange Horsemen and other abductions. But that was many weeks distance for most in the south and not of immediate concern. At any rate, according to Southlanders, *who, in their right mind, would traverse the routes bordering the Northland anyway? They must be foolish souls! Almost deserving what they encountered. After all, these were the risks of travelers since the Separation War!*

After the Separation War the Gotts were given back the limits of their barren rugged territory. The mountains to the east, Lake of Choices to the south, the Burning Forest to the west and the Ice Barrens of the North...a veritable prison! There seemed enough physical separation to allow the rest of the worlds to live in bliss, or so it was thought.

There is more to protection though, than barriers. For even the strongest barrier was no match for the lingering power of Lord Ho. Thank the heavens he was gone, but what of the Magic? Where did it go? Surely that was all over long ago? There had been so much peace since then, that most had forgotten those days of power, war and the Magic of the Old Ones. Most remembrances of those times were now relegated to scary bedtime stories or threats: *'The Gotts will get you! They lurk in the darkness, and wait for stray bad children, who don't listen to their elders. They wait and then gobble them up, never to be seen again!'* Those days were gone?

Why were the Gotts digging? Who were the

Horsemen? It was accepted that the Gotts used slave labor and that most of their captives were the homeless; so it was easy to ignore. The strange Horsemen riding more and more southward should have sent out the alert. What was so precious that all other Gott priorities had fallen aside in order to allow this digging to be rapidly accomplished? These were to remain unanswered until it was too late.

The main activity of the digging was taking place in Norkleau. Norkleau was the original seat of power for the centuries of the Old Ones. Ruins lay upon ruins and it was said that under it all was a great secret; the true magic and power that had eluded and destroyed Lord Ho. For Lord Ho had summoned the Magic of the Lake of Choices, not realizing the source from which it truly came! He would regret calling it forth!

Many centuries ago the Lake's edge and Norkleau had been joined, but time and drought had gradually done its part in their severing on the surface, though below ground a series of caverns and rivers flowed back and forth between the two.

Norkleau had slipped into the control of the Gotts more out of disinterest than any other reason. It was of no strategic value; neither economic nor political. If the Gotts wanted the barren territory and ruins, they were welcome to them. If it kept them occupied and not warring with the South, fine!

The Gotts until recently, also shared this disinterest in Norkleau, until their new leader 'Merm', had taken command after a bloody murderous rampage. This rid him of all competitors, which was the Gott custom and therefore no cause for outside alarm.

Merm had taken control over a year before my first meeting with 'D'. He brought rapid changes, including a heretofore unknown prosperity to the normally poor scavenging Gotts. He was loved, he was feared, cruel and dirty, having kinked long hair and a beard. You could smell him before you saw him and when you set eyes upon his warty nine foot body, you realized that this was the archetypal Gott of old.

In coming to power Merm had gained access to the Forbidden Books. These were the chronicles of the Gott, containing the history and secrets learnt and guardedly passed on from Lord to Lord. It had been more a symbol of office, till Merm. For Lord Merm had mastered the tongue of the Forbidden script and upon its reading was lured by the references to powerful *Passwords of Promise* and descriptions of the Old Ones. These ancients had found the meaning and ways of invincibility. They had written their discoveries through magic {Passwords of Promise} and left a Key, to which the possessor would be given all knowing power and control of the Magic of the Lake of Choices. How could Merm use such strengths? He could regain the rightful position of the Gotts, and enslave the three worlds! But where was this Key?

From his Keep in Aug, Lord Merm had searched and reread every document he could lay his eyes upon. Till finally there it was, in the Fifth Book of Ho! The Key was to be found in the Palace of the Lake of Choices. There were three warnings or conditions depending upon the way you took the translation, but Merm couldn't wait till he properly deciphered them. He decided go to Norkleau and start the search, leaving the job of translation till after he had started the digging. He would take the Fifth book along, and finish both jobs together. After all, the hardest part was already accomplished—the discovery of the location of the Key, or so he thought.

"There look! Another found is! That four make this week. Quickly, before he out is of Forest! Receive we will great honor when Lord Merm of our abilities hears to him supply the labor for Gott dig! A bonus to one who captures him not damaged!"

The Horsemen rode off in pursuit of yet another victim. But this was no ordinary quarry.

'D' was on her way to Jard for the Summer Festival. She had decided to go by way of the Burning Forest. It would be a day out of her way, but there were stories of abductions and disappearances she wanted to investigate.

She had left three days before from her home in Loto, just to the south of the Gott Mountains in the foothills. It had been a beautiful hike along the southern shores of the Lake and now, after her observations, she would take the Western Path through the tip of the lower Forest and then turn southeast heading for Jard. In another two days she would arrive in time for the celebrations.

As she hiked, she recalled her meeting five years before, of the Stoneman's son; it seemed a long time ago. She began to recall another Stoneman's son. She remembered the joy, the strong smile and the sweetness of the man she had loved. But they were of different kinds. She was of the Old Ones, and he not. She never revealed this, nor her love, for it was not permitted. It had been so lonely till then, and now again. That was the curse of the Old Ones. In order to enjoy longevity and magical power you must know that you would watch all others pass beyond, leaving you to your memories and sometimes anguish.

To be of the Old Ones was a special honor. Only few were chosen and fewer still passed the 'test of deservedness'. She was, and she had, so long ago now. As far as she knew, she was the last of the Old Ones. In the fighting of the Separation War, all the others had been captured, tortured and killed. She had managed to survive and kept concealed her true nature. For those of the Old Ones were responsible for the balance of good and evil, power and magic. It was their duty to quietly watch and guard against evil doers, such as Lord Ho. But the battle with Ho had drained their numbers to virtual extinction. The Magic of the Lake had been used, and in order to re-establish the Balance, many sacrifices had been made. 'D' was now worried that all the recent disappearances might be early indications that something was again tapping into and disturbing the Balance. She had felt tremors in the Magic. If something was beginning, now was the time to find out. Maybe she would be enough to stop any early problems.

As all these thoughts meandered through her mind, 'D' was unaware of the approaching Horsemen. Without any warning from behind and to her right, there was the crashing sound of something wild approaching through the woods. 'D' jarred back to ready herself, scanning in the direction of the sounds with ears, sight, and smell. There was trouble brewing. Every instinct in her being was preparing her for flight or fight, depending on the threat. She placed her left hand on her jeweled sword, both a gift and her symbol. She felt reassured. *"Magic and my right."* Or in her case left, was spoken under her breath. It was the battle cry of the Old Ones.

"Hasn't anything been found yet?!" shouted Lord Merm. He was tired and frustrated. He had not slept much since his arrival in Norkleau and had spent most of his time here, in his chambers, agonizing over the Fifth Book of Ho. "There should be some indication by now. I know I am right. It's got to be here!" he pounded a large finger on the big leather bound book upon the table.

"But Lord, we have been digging for weeks and..."

"SILENCE!" Merm cut off his Troop Commander. "I *will* have results. Now! Double the numbers on the dig crews."

"But Lord, we already are working the slaves too hard. We need fresh...

"Then get the slaves you need, and tell those accursed Horsemen there is a great reward for the Riders with the best results. They will receive the greatest privileges under my rule. Now get out!"

The Troop Commander turned and hurried out of the chamber, leaving Merm alone. As he left, Merm wondered why was he surrounded by such incompetents!

The Lord was upset not only at the lack of results in the digging, but also by the incomplete translation of the first warning:

'Beware the lady of the jewel.
She fully awakens at the first . . .'

and that was it. He couldn't break the rest of the words. He was frustrated and making no headway. He decided that he was too fatigued and must rest. Maybe after he was calm it would come to him.

Merm hadn't expected the warning, it caught him off guard. In his obsessiveness he wondered if he had overlooked an important step. Was this the type of mistake Lord Ho had made? What did it all mean? He was too close to risk losing all on some female. Or was it just a trap? Yes, that must be it!

"Rmont! Commander Rmont come here at once! I believe we must go and see for ourselves what is being dug. We must be careful of the first uncovering. Rmont!"

Merm excitedly left his conference chamber in search of his Commander, pleased with this newest insight.

Flight would be the most clever move at this point, for if the worst was to happen then who would be left to watch? The Old Ones may live a long time, but they were not immortal!

'D' jumped off the path away from the noise and scurried into the forest.

"After him!" came a low raspy voice. "Over there! In wood is!"

The chase was on, but the Horsemen knew not their

quarry and would be easily mislead. Down the hill into the thick bramble and briars; no horse would follow — but they did!

"Who are these strange riders?" thought 'D' as she ran through the prickly escape route. Panicking, she fell, caught her tunic on something, struggled, and heard the 'rrrrip' as she rose to rush on. It was followed, almost immediately, by the quick thud and pain of a cross arrow piercing her side. She was hit but not badly. She was only wounded. She grabbed her lower right side and yes, there it was, a stick-like object imbedded in her. She held her side and continued the escape.

The Horsemen were from the Ice Barrens and of the nomadic tribes. They were for hire and would show allegiance to whosoever bid the most reward. They particularly enjoyed this type of mission. They were simply mercenaries, and lived that lifestyle. To the strong the spoils, was their only credo. They were strong and they were good. The more risky the challenge the better they succeeded.

As she continued to run, 'D' began to see that the trouble in the North was more than just a small band of ruffians terrorizing the pathways. There was a strong magic swelling forth, and a threat to the three worlds! There was only one tribe willing or able to hire these Riders—the Gotts! Lord Merm was up to no good!

"Got-ya! Little rabbit."

She was surrounded.

"Ah...Rmont there you are. Where were you? We have work to do at the dig." The two marched off.

The digging had gone through many layers of time. Now everyone around the dig watched, as the original city level approached. The spot picked for the dig had depended upon the particular interpretation of the ancient lore, for the Palace was said to be: *'neath the 'Shrine of the Stars'*. All had agreed finally, that the location of the Shrine of the Stars, was under the old pillared amphitheater that was in a knoll in the center of the city. Every effort was now being placed at this site.

The city of Norkleau resembled an earthquake zone with: piles of rubble, half finished holes from earlier digging and collapsed buildings, all over. It was no longer a very pretty town but it was said that in the days of the Old Ones it was a sparkling center for all the worlds. Now Norkleau merely served as a mythical center upon which legend had come to rest.

There was quite a bustle going on around the Shrine as Lord Merm arrived, followed closely by Rmont.

"Report!" demanded the Lord of his captain in charge of the Shrine dig as he came within voice range.

"My Lord. We seem to have found a door…about sixty lengths down. It is certainly of the Old Ones making, but we are unable to move it. It appears to be made of solid rock."

"Good…good Captain, you have pleased me. Now call the slaves out and let us have a closer look."

"Yes, my Lord Merm. Thank you my Lord Merm," turning to face the pit behind him, the Captain addressed those below. "Right, everyone out! Make room for the Lord Merm!"

There was a rapid exodus and then the Lord's party descended into the cavernous dig.

"So, what we here have?" questioned the head Rider, "Hert wench little. Tell name traveler!"

There was no answer, for just as 'D' began to speak she felt a crack on her head and she collapsed.

"What do that fer? Want know who is brave wench," blurted out the head Rider to a large fellow Rider who had hit 'D' harder than he expected.

"Jus want make her not waste re time. She made me her damage with cross arrow. Lord Merm no want slaves damaged before deliver to his Troops," replied Tan.

"Bring wench. We stay night in spot here."

The six other Riders dismounted and began to make preparations for the night.

"Tan. You fix hurt wench. Maybe we trick the Gotts." The head Rider gave out what might be considered a laugh.

When 'D' awoke she was tied to a tree and twenty lengths or so away, were the Riders, huddled around a small smokeless fire laughing and talking about their experiences. 'D' was trying to think of an escape and was only half listening when she overheard them speak the 'name'.

"*Lord Merm* pleased will be with all new slaves. Him they help get power and magic more. He soon find secret place of Old."

So, that was it! Lord Merm had discovered the secret, and somehow had learned of a possible location of the Magic. That's why all the new commotion in the North. Lord Merm was going to create an imbalance and try to dominate the worlds as Lord Ho had tried. This time, Merm would have the invincible magic of the Old Ones. She must escape and stop Merm from acquiring the Magic hidden in the Lost Palace. She hoped it wouldn't be too late.

'D' knew of the legends and had once been told of an entrance to the hiding place of power, near the Lake of Choices, but she never realized that there still existed the Key. Merm must be stopped! The Key had no power by itself, but whoever possessed it, could use it to unlock the power of good or evil.

'D' now remembered the cross arrow and felt for it in her side. It was gone and a moist salve was covering the wound. She momentarily felt gratitude for the medical attention, but then quickly turned her mind to finding a way out of this mess.

"My sword. If only I could see it."

As 'D' spoke to herself, she gave a visual sweep of the camp from left to right and then, there it was, a glisten in the firelight! She decided to wait till these oafs drifted one by one to sleep before she attempted to retrieve the sword. So assured were these Riders of their prowess, that no guards were posted.

Eventually when they were all asleep, 'D' closed her eyes and hummed a beautiful tune. It was almost a lullaby it was so sweet. As she hummed, her eyes re-opened and she fixed her thoughts on her sword. Slowly the weapon began to shimmer and move towards her. It was a long effort, but finally, sword by her side, 'D' cut her ropes and was on her way to free-dom.

From deep within the pit in Norkleau, Lord Merm beamed, "Ah...I see, this must be the way! Well done Captain, extra rations and a week's reward to your corp."

Merm examined the rock door closely, noticing every detail and scratch. He would have to wait for now and discover the meaning of the first warning before venturing beyond or tampering with the door. He must be careful!

"Seal this area and guard it well, I will return to my chamber and solve the remaining warnings."

"Immediately, my Lord." as he answered, the Captain ushered his Troops to comply with their Lord's wishes. They all bowed their heads and held a clenched hand over their forehead as Merm and his entourage returned to the surface.

Chapter 3.

It was a spacious room with one ceiling to floor arched window overlooking the south west. The Lake was just visible in the distance and below encamped, were nothing but Troops and mess. Each stone in its walls had been hand fitted and were thick as an arm length in all directions. The stone was a tanish color and gave a warmth to the otherwise bare decoration of the room. In the middle was a large oak table and a chair with a figure bent over mumbling and scribbling over and over. There was parchment everywhere and still more to follow. The feather quills of spent pens lay here and there. Only the spiral stairway on the western wall seemed to be going anywhere.

At the top of the heavy stone stairs was a thick and large round door, which if opened lead down a corridor and into the main hall … *The Great Hall of Omift.*

Merm had been here for hours trying to understand the words and then the double meaning of the fifth Forbidden Book. He wasn't pleased with his lack of progress. The Troops were becoming restless, how much longer would it be before he could lead them on their conquering journey south to the first of the three worlds? He didn't want to rush and make mistakes that would later cause much unneeded trouble.

'Beware the lady of the jewel. She fully awakens at the first . . .'

What was the next word? Sound? Tune? What could it mean? Which lady? Was she alive, or some guardian

18

set to react when an intruder entered past the rock
door? These old words of warning had come from the
experience of his predecessors and so heeding their
wisdom was important. But the 'Lady' of the jewel?
What did it all mean?

Merm continued the search to find any reference that
would add light to the phrase. His thoughts turned to
the rock door at the dig and the engravings upon it.
There was a statue of two seated colossal men; between them a passage and a sword with little bumps on
its pommel. There was also a sun in the upper left corner. Three figures formed an arch shape at the top of
the door and what appeared to be a female with long
hair was below them. Merm thought out loud: "Could
these have something to do with the warning?"

At that moment a knocking sounded upon the sturdy
oak door, momentarily distracting his thoughts.

"Enter!" the Lord commanded.

The door creaked noise as it slowly opened its full
width to reveal several uniformed Troops and Rmont.

"Sir, Lord Merm. Lieutenant Blag, to report on the
Riders and their slave complements. I think we have a
very impressive Riding here, who have earned an audience," suggested Rmont, realizing that this would
distract the Troops and make them less restless, after
hearing of the success and ability of these hired ar-
rows.

"Well,… you think, do you? Don't overstep your
place, I will decide on such matters!"

"Oh, yes Lord… but," Rmont approached so as to be
beyond the hearing of the others. "This is just the type
of distraction we need, till we can mobilize the rest of
the Troops to your glorious conquest. Until the warnings are deciphered and entrance through the rock door
permitted." Rmont paused, he had made his point
clear. For whenever a large Troop is gathered and is
restless; morale and loyalty dwine. This would certainly secure some more time before the Troops became unmanageable.

"Yes...Yes report then!" Merm had understood.

Rmont motioned one of the escorting Gott Officers to proceed.

"Lord," commenced Lieutenant Blag. "May I present to you sir, the Head Rider, 'Gorg' of Ice Barrens."

"Good honor sir Lord, I bring many helpy slave for you to work. Forty-nine numbers but one wenchy got away with magic sword, she had..."

Merm had only been half listening, expecting this to be a meaningless report from what he had always thought a stupid dirty tribe. They had their place when you had a need, but no other possible value. Their inability to properly speak, irritated him.

"What!...Wenchy what...magic sword...explain yourself!"

The outburst had been so unexpected that even Rmont drew back in surprise and fear.

"Sorry Lord. No mean hert wenchy,...but away did get. Had flying sword did she. Too smart she was. Next time tie her good I will."

"Where was this and when?" Merm pushed.

"One nights camp before Norkleau, my Lord Merm," cowered Gorg the Rider. For though Riders were a fearless tribe, the one thing they disliked most was non payment of agreed reward or bonuses. Gorg was concerned that missing this one slave might cause the Gott leader to renege on the promised rewards and favored position. So he continued to try and appease his employer, and answered the other questions that were presented.

Merm had yet another of his realizations. Perhaps there was a connection between the events of the female of Gorg's account and that of the first warning! He must find out. He must have the female and her 'magic flying' sword. Maybe these were clues to the other warnings. Certainly if what Gorg had recounted was true, then it would be wise to investigate further.

"I want that female, *here*, and with this sword you speak of."

"Know not where wenchy go. Can guess only." whined Gorg, who was also angered at the foolishness of Tan on the night of the capture {Tan was to check the captives, but forgot}. This might cost. He would deal with Tan later, but first the Gott leader needed to be soothed. "Will find and here bring right away, my Lord Merm."

"Good, my little friend. I give you till weeks end to prove your value to the Gott. Make no mistake to bring the female alive, or I will have heads! Lieutenant Blag. Take twelve of your men and make certain my wishes are completed."

Merm turned away and by a wave of his arm dis- missed them all. He returned to his table and started writing down notes.

After the long nights flee through the bramble and wood of the lower Burning Forest, 'D' happened upon a pathway. She hoped it was going south and that the Horsemen were nowhere near. She continued the trek, never meeting a soul, which was odd at this festive time of season. Though Jard was still at least a days travel, there should be interest in the Festival displayed even this far north! Putting these thoughts aside, she looked upward as she walked. The day was getting dark with unusual clouds approaching from over the northeast, from over the Lake of Choices.

Choices, what an appropriate name. Any northward traveler coming upon the Lake would stop, and con- sider their route. Without a boat, the Lake was impos- sible to cross and even upon crossing was treacherous, with its sudden storms arising and going out of nowhere. That was not a choice for most. Or to the east the Gott Mountains, again a difficult journey with many smelly Gotts just awaiting. The Burning Forest was the choice of most, but that too, as you know, now had its dangers. The only other choice was to simply return from whence you had come and not continue in the Northland direction! Destiny was always at hand at the Lake. So naturally its name had developed.

By evening of her day of escape 'D' was a little lost and hungry. The small rations that she always carried, were not designed for this type of arduous travel. She was in need of food and rest. As she progressed, the pathway led her into a clearing. 'D' noticed through the early dusk, smoke rising from a chimney of a lone building off in the distance ahead. It was Colleg's tavern. She had never been there before, but knew of its existence along the northern path. The appearance of the tavern surprised her, for she hadn't realized that she had come this far northwest in her escape from the Horsemen. Certainly it would be safe to stop awhile and sup. "Ah!" she noted. "I will try this little tavern. Something smells good."

The Old One crossed the distance quickly and soon entered onto the quaint dimly lit stone terrace in the front of the tavern. No one seemed to be here, but the smell of dinner being prepared did not allow her thoughts to linger long on the absence. She went to the entrance, turned the large cast iron handle and pushed open the heavy door, stepping across and into a smoky, musty, fire lit room.

There were steps leading down towards a bar in front of her and to the right a room with tables ready for customers.

"Greetings weary traveler! Welcome to my home. Sit. Drink. You have arrived in time for sup!"

A rotund figure from behind the bar was beckoning her in and toward one of the empty tables. Why was no one else here? Was it just the recent trouble that had scared all away, or was there something else? 'D' continued to reconnoiter. Finally she paid attention to the plump jovial figure that hadn't stopped jabbering since her arrival.

"It is good to have company on such a dreary eve. Where are you headed? I'll bet the Jard Festival!?"

'D' shrugged in acknowledgment. Normally she

would have been more careful of questions delivered in this manner, but she was tired, weak and hungry. Her wound was healing but sore. She moved to one of the tables, and found the attempt to sit awkward. Her side still panged and she was distracted by its sudden renewal of sharp pain.

The innkeeper noticed, and without mentioning his awareness continued: "I will get you food and drink. Will you rest here tonight?"

'Will you rest here tonight rang in her head?'...No. It didn't feel safe. Mingled within her thoughts a voice was warning: *"Eat, drink and then go! Do not stay long!"* Was it the tavern or some other following danger? She did not know. It had been so long since her training and the instincts of the Old Ones were used.

"Thank you kind sir." She was perturbed but tried not to show it to this curious innkeeper.

"Please, I am called Colleg."

"Colleg, thank you for your hospitality, but I must continue my journey, now that I am so close to Jard. The Festival begins tomorrow and I must be there by early eve, or I shall lose my place."

"What, pray tell, will you do at the Festival?" inquired Colleg.

"Sell my crafts and herbs."

As she spoke, she realized that her bag was no longer with her. It must have been lost during her capture by the Horsemen. No!...They would now know her. But why would that matter? She was merely a 'wenchy' traveler. Inside of her an uneasiness arose, and her urgency to continue the journey grew. She quickly covered: "I have left my bag with a friend and it would not be wise, during the Festival, to delay longer."

"Fine, my lady. Food and drink it is then. The best for our guest!" with that Colleg left to prepare the meal.

It had been the best meal in a long time, but now it was only a pleasant memory to carry her on as she now continued her walk. She had eaten ravenously and without acknowledgment of the conversation that Colleg attempted to make. When she had finally finished her last bite of food and a tankard of drink, she realized that she hadn't considered the price for all that she had consumed. Placing her hand in her pocket, she was pleased to find that she fortunately had what she felt, was more than enough money to pay for the meal. She had asked for the accounting, paid and then quickly left. Now she was well on her way south! Only a few more hours and then by early eve, Jard. The meal had returned much energy, and the pain in her side was diminishing.

Jard. In the rush to escape, 'D' neglected to notice how all her actions since, were of a subconscious origin. She was being driven towards Jard rapidly and it wasn't just by the Festival. There were other forces involved. Deep within her a reawakening was in progress. Ever since the utterance of the Old Ones battle cry and the melody of power, which was a harmless trick she had used many times in the past to either find her sword or simply amuse, much more appeared to be happening. She must hurry. She realized she was going to meet people of importance. Someone or ones whose secret had, like moles, dug in deeply, to lie dormant and hidden till a time of calling, although this knowledge had not, as of yet, fully surfaced nor was it consciously understood. The Old Ones within could no longer sleep!

After the disastrous meeting with the Lord Merm, Gorg displayed his foul temper when he and his Riders had managed to clear the city wall of Norkleau. They were to wait there till Lieutenant Blag and his contingent arrived. Meanwhile he would deal with Tan. This would remind his other Riders to mind their actions and voice. He rode up to Tan and pushed the Rider from his mount.

"Oi…!" exclaimed Tan as he thundered downward.

"Stupid horseless Rider. Have not you mind. That wenchy valuable is to Gott. Gave you no thought to my word. We now must find or lose reward! Where we find…his wenchy and her metal…eh?…smart one! What say?! Now not so smart…Eh!" Gorg peered down at the embarrassed Rider. There was light fearful laughter from the others who were not willing to challenge Gorg or alienate Tan.

"Having fun I was. Only wenchy!" stuttered Tan.

"Only wenchy Merm want. Now how find?" questioned Gorg.

Tan fell silent and paused to think, then a smile began to rise up his face.

"Know where find do I, Gorg sir. Traveler leave belonging in wood. Know where is. I find belonging. It tell where wenchy be!" Tan was very pleased with himself, for now Gorg would be happy, and forgive this big lout for his childish play, and he, Tan, would not lose much face with the others. The confrontation was over and all felt properly entertained. The rest of the Riders then dismounted and proceeded to refresh their horses and catch a short rest, while they awaited Blag. It would be their only rest before the long hard ride back to the forest.

From within the castle room at Norkleau there came a joyful noise:

"That's it! Of course:

**'Beware the Lady and the jewel.
She fully awakens at the first sound of the rock door's Tune.'**

"But what does it mean? The other warnings must

reveal more. Just as I thought, this female is connected. I must question her soon. Now is the time to open that door, and then after, continue this accursed decipherment!"

Merm rose and proceeded to dress. The door would be opened by early eve. So the conquest begins! He felt the nearness of the Key with all its powerful magic. He wondered if the Lord Ho had had the same premonitions of greatness and power. The nearness of which one could almost touch. How he hoped that the other two warnings would be simpler and less mystifying. Regardless, he could endure. The decoding of the first warning had given him new found confidence in the rightness of his evil motive.

"Harder! Put your backs into it! Put another bar on this side. Now heave! Heave! Heave! Whew, this is a hard one. Must be rusted up."

"It can't be rusted. It's made of a type of stone."

"You know what I mean. It's just been sitting too long untouched. Here, slide one of the bars around the opening cracks to see if we have missed a latch or stopper of some kind."

"Attention!" cried the Unit Guard. "The Lord Merm approaches!"

As Merm arrived he spoke out: "As you were. How is the opening, Captain? Will we get into whatever lies beyond, this eve?"

"Certainly Lord. Only a push or pull and you will be able to enter."

"Fine. Good work Troopers. Keep it going. Show me that my Troops are invincible!" encouraged Merm out loud so all in the area could overhear.

Again the Troopers pried and again the door remained as it had been for all these centuries.

"Sir. There seems to be a protuberance of some kind at the bottom corner. Shall I try the bar on it?" called out one of the Troopers helping at the rock door.

"Excellent Trooper! You have done well before your Lord. Yes, pry the bar between the rock and whatever that is.

Again the Troopers all heaved as the one pried. Again, and again....POP....zzzzzzzclick.

"Sir we have it...............Now heave!"

The door began to move. It sounded heavy and the dirt crushed as the door rolled to its full opening. Once the door was wide open there emanated a sound. It was very high pitched and only six or seven notes. No it was more a melody. But so high and penetrating that all in the vicinity covered their ears and drew back in fearful anticipation.

It was the tune of the warning. Merm was startled and wondered who this tune according to the warning would awaken.

"What do you see Captain?" the Lord impatiently questioned.

The Captain cautiously peered in past the rock door opening while the others kept back and away. The sound of the tune had alarmed them.

"A corridor my Lord. A long passageway. We will need ropes and torches."

"See to it. We embark to the Lost Palace within the hour!" Merm was exultant!

———————————————

'D' awoke from her short rest. She had felt uneasy more than fatigued, so she decided to take the snooze. She was only a matter of two or three hours from the outskirts of Jard, therefore the stop would cause little harm. During her rest she had been plagued by dreams of pursuers, with glowing red eyes of evil power. She didn't appreciate the meaning, for at the same time from deep within, a voice was calling. It seemed to want something. It came from the past, not hers, but that of the Old. It had eagerness in its tone but the words were not distinguishable. There also seemed to be a slight hint of music. Uncertainty ran through her.

She must reach Jard. *Why Jard?* There was no answer, just the imperative feeling to make the destination before it became too late. Questioning made no difference, acceptance appeared the only process that kindled any kind of peace within. Time was flowing out, no longer in sync with the worlds. The center of balance had been tipped, causing what might best be described as a fast steady leak. All goodness being sucked into an abyss.

Rising, 'D' gave herself a thorough shake in an effort to re-establish the focal point of her reality—to no avail. The urgency of the inner voice was growing. She must hurry, and so she commenced her last leg of the journey to Jard.

Jard, an unusually hard sounding name for a village of such quaint inhabitants and picturesqueness. A village known for toleration and peace, where there was still time to chat with friends and not feel obligated to rush to and fro. Every cottage was clean and every garden plush. Jardians took pride in their reputation as the best planters in all the worlds. If 'D' was to pick a paradise on the planets, she would have no other choice. It was Jard. She thought about this pleasantness till finally she had arrived at Jard. The time had flown by without much notice on her part.

As she entered the village her memory returned to the many visits she had made over the years. The Summer Festivals. The long evenings of conversation and tea. Tea, bread and jam. Tea, bread and jam. How sweet the thought. Suddenly 'D' knew where she must go:

"Julian!...Yes I must go to tea on the path at Julians', that is why I came!...Yes how foolish I didn't see earlier. The Stoneman's son...Julian!"

Renewed energy filled her bones. She set off to find the Stoneman's son's cottage. It was getting late in the afternoon, so she would have to be snappy!

- - - - - - - - - - - - - - - -

Down the path through the center of the village 'D' hurried. Everywhere were crowds for the Festival. They looked happier than other times. How nice to be back amongst the normal! A wave here, a greeting there, no one was unwelcomed.

Within a very small distance Julian's cottage materialized. He was home, if the smoke emanating from the chimney was a reliable indicator. 'D' went onto his path and said to herself: "Well he did invite me to tea," and advanced toward the front door.

Obtaining no result from her knock, she decided the best place to find a Jardian was, of course, in his garden. Around the side of the cottage she leapt, swinging the gate open and closed with a loud clang. Two amazed young villagers and Julian were standing. 'D', seeing she was in time for tea, shouted out in greeting tone, her order.

"Gorg! Looky. Find wenchy belonging I have!"

The Riders had galloped through the night and searched by the lower end of the Burning Forest for the bramble and briar, the place where they had first caught and wounded 'D', two nights before. It wasn't a difficult job, since the Riders were keen trackers and could easily retrace their steps. The worry was whether or not the bag had already been found by another in the woods. This thought had driven them. Tan let out a sigh of relief, now that it was found. Surely there would be something inside to lead them on to the wench's recapture.

Gorg was handed the belonging and tore through it without regard. Throwing whatever he encountered to the ground. Herbs, plants, toiletries, and some wenchy under things. That was all!

"What wenchy kind this is!" Gorg exclaimed. For any other woman would have carried much more, he felt certain. This was a strange situation. He wondered what was so special about this one. Perhaps he would find even greater reward from others for this wenchy. The Riders were at a loss at finding nothing of importance.

"Here. Show it to me." demanded the Lieutenant. Blag was handed the bag and its belongings. "There is much to tell still. Ask yourself why would a person carry so many plants? They must be medicinal, and at this time of year why carry them on the pathways? The Summer Festival of Jard. That is the destination of our female. Let us proceed through the area and think like the female. She would be in need of food, drink and rest. There is only one such place within a days walk. Colleg's tavern. I know this area well, and that is our next stop. Gorg, Tan, you will know this female if you see her?"

"Rider never forget," answered Tan.

"Splendid. Then it is only a matter of 'when' we find the female, not 'if'."

Blag threw the bag to the ground. He was pleased to show up the Riders with his tracking skills. Without uttering another word, he rode off in the direction of the tavern. It was still a ways off, but each member of the party knew now, that they could easily track this female and were only a day or so ride behind. The tracks would be fresh and the memories of those they would question, still vivid.

The Lieutenant's party rode ahead. Gorg beckoned his Riders and quietly leaned towards them.

"No like this Gott. Must careful be. No trust. Will take our reward for himself. At right timing we control will take. Now for we wait and use till the wenchy safe in Riders' mount."

The ride would be long again. There would be no rest until the recapture.

If only 'D' was aware of her fate, but maybe she was. Maybe she was already beginning to become awakened to these dangers.

Chapter 4.

"It took me some time to understand the strangeness about these days. After my present journey, I have seen many wrong signs, and within me is a stirring. I will tell you that great danger is about to surface, and that all the worlds will be in the greatest of danger. Riders are scavenging the Northlands, and certainly will venture southward, sooner than we may like. The Gotts are preparing to war again with the South. They have discovered secrets of Old and I believe will soon find the legends of the Lost Palace to be true. There is a *Key* to protect and *Passwords of Promise* to keep from the control of the evil that starts its spread. I am not yet knowledgeable in all the reasons, or the part we shall each play, but it involves all of us. It is locked away in us till the need has arisen, thereby protecting ourselves by our ignorance.

I will tell you what I know. When the time is upon us, a sign will unlock that which lies deep ... "

'D' began to lose track of her speech and heard a distant sound, six maybe seven notes. She had never heard the notes before but something inside recognized their meaning.

Julian, Thiunn, and Eruinn also felt the sounds and a stirring deep within.

"What's happening?" called out one of the young-sters.

"DO NOT BE CONCERNED CHOSEN ONE!"

It was an ancient voice, and all four had heard it, but the two young villagers thought that only they could hear.

Coupled with their earlier amazement from 'D's entrance in the red shirt, Julian and his nephews began to now notice that the jewels in the sword were glowing brighter and brighter, and that 'D' herself was being enveloped by a whitish egg shaped glow, like an aura. It kept growing till finally the sword stopped glowing and merely hummed.

"Do not be concerned Chosen Ones!"

Now the voice emanated from 'D' herself, in fact, it was her own voice but stronger in tone and impact:

"The door is past. The evil begins.
Awaken! Begin! Four shall defend.
Beware of the power, the Stoneman's flight.
Two are deserving, in the Lake test their rights,
All was forgotten and now comes true.
A mason, two children, a woman,
All know the old tune.
The evil has power to capture the Key.
Passwords of Promise remain to be freed.
In the city of sparkle under the stars,
Return to your birthright and balance them all."

The six notes pierced through each of them and then there was sudden blackness!

Eruinn was the first to awaken, and quickly roused his brother, Uncle and then 'D'. They had obviously passed out under the shrill noise. For how long was uncertain, but it was now night, and they were all still in the garden in Jard.

"'D'. Are you all right? Is everyone okay?" checked Eruinn.

"Oh... What a day this has been! Strange Horsemen, the Gotts and this!" 'D' was mumbling as she began to come 'round.

"Had I known this was going to happen, I never would have offered you tea all those years ago!" Julian was still a little stunned and it was difficult to determine if he was making a humorous or serious statement. 'D' ignored the words.

"Thiunn, rise and shine. Let's all go into the cottage. There are plans to make and details to explain." 'D' led the way into the little home.

They all made their way through the cottage and sat in a cozy room facing the west of the property, warmed by the large impressive fireplace. 'D' started:

"I am called Darla, my title {for even now she must not reveal that she was of the Old Ones} is Princess. I am the last of my line of the Palace of Norkleau. Deep within, we have secrets as to our purpose. I know that Julian is a Stoneman, like his father and his father before him. The Stonemen were the protectors of the Key in ancient times and only they were incorruptible by its power and promises. It was they who hid the Key and safeguarded its use by wrongdoers. Julian it is your task, once the Key is found, to return it to safe keeping away from the Gotts and Lord Merm. I only hope we are not too late, for once Merm has control of the Key, it will be up to Eruinn, Thiunn and myself to regain the power and destroy the Gott leader. It would be a difficult task. The *Evil* is strong.

Eruinn, and Thiunn, are Chosen, and must pass the test of deservedness. If you fail you will perish. The test will be part of the quest we will embark upon this very night. If you succeed you will become the youngest Chosen in a very long time, and likely never use the magic you will soon learn, again, after this quest is through. If we are not successful, the *evil* dark will be spread by the Lord Merm, and then even he will become slave to that cruel master. We will be lost along with all the worlds. We must not let that happen!

I can tell you only this, and these words are not to pass to any other. You are sworn on peril of death. There is no choice. Only the completion of the calling.

Do not ask me why, for there is not an answer. You two have been Chosen, and Julian has a birth right and duty, like his fathers and sons before him."

"But... who are we, we're just young villagers?" both nephews complained.

"There is no reason. The choice is made. The test is all that remains."

With that they fell to silence. Julian who had not said a word to this point, was thinking of his father and the long talks and stories he used to laboriously tell, always asking his son if he would swear to do his part when the time came. Julian thought his father meant family responsibilities and the passing on of the craft. But now he reasoned that this Key was also a part of the responsibility. He had heard stories of ancient magic and the important mission to protect the Balance. He now realized that they were not just stories, but also his father's way of protecting the son from the knowledge itself. It would cause danger should he be too aware of details. His father must have known that when the voice spoke during a time of need, that it would then all be made clear, and it was!

"How do we go and what do we take?" asked Julian of Princess Darla.

"We will begin before dawn and take one set of: clothing, food, drink, rope, a knife each, and courage. No one must know of our purpose or destination. No one!"

"But there will be great fear upon our disappearance and my sister will worry when these two do not return this eve. We must...

"No one must know! When we return, if we return, then there will be reason to tell. If we are prevented from our task there will be no one left to worry."

There were so many questions to ask, and the Princess would answer some, but to others:

"You will know when the need is shown. Trust yourselves. Listen to what is in you. Relax and just be. I have confidence that the right choices have been made already."

It still didn't really satisfy. Everything was all so un-foreseen, isn't that always the way. What you want you never get, not when you need; or, what you don't want you get too much of, especially when you don't need.

It was crazy. It was time. Julian accepted the role his father had prepared him for, and the two young Chosen Ones welcomed this both as a grown up adventure and a teenage nightmare. How could they refuse? Even if there had been a choice on their part? Their mother had always said that their Uncle would lead them to no good. Wouldn't she be delighted by all this!

The questioning would never have stopped if not for the Princess's concern that the Lord Merm was on the move and that by now spies would be about. She felt certain that Merm would also have felt the disturbance in the Balance, and would be anxious not to delay. Perhaps he was also knowledgeable to the existence of the 'four to defend'. If so, he would be on the look-out, maybe even have sent Troops after these four.

"We had better all get ready. There isn't much time before dawn. Pack your things in a small bag and then get some rest. We depart in two hours. Remember stay near and speak to no one."

Not that anyone was around at this moment of the early morning.

'D', rather Darla, noticed her side was beginning to pain. She needed some rest, especially after the events of the past hours. She considered a brief itinerary. They would travel northward to the Lake of Choices, and once there, enter the secret passageway and even-tually the Lost Palace. She hoped again it wasn't too late. And what about the Horsemen and the Gotts? It would be hard to avoid them, but they must. The longer their presence was questionable to the Lord, the better chance there would be to surprise and not cause alarm to the evil, which could force its early hand.

If only she had foreseen all this months ago! Things hadn't been right, even she had known that much. Hind sight, there was no point in dwelling on the past possibilities. Now the time was at hand and something would be done, even with these three, whose inexperience worried Darla. Why had they been selected? Of course there was no answer. She should just trust the picking. She shrugged it off and decided to get some rest.

In another room in the cottage, one of the nephews was placing a note on a table. It wouldn't hurt. He didn't think anyone but the housekeeper would find it and then deliver it to his mother. He didn't like the idea of her worrying about their absence. What possible harm could it bring? He kept it secret. No need to involve the others. They would only think him a child.

- - - - - - - - - - - - - - - - - -

The moment of departure had arrived. The door was closed and the outside porch gas light left on. No one saw them leave. They headed over the back garden fence and into the meadow, heading northward. They would try to avoid the festivities by taking a longer route around the village.

Within an hour they were well out of sight of Jard. They each prayed that they would be fortunate and return to see this lovely home again soon, and that all would be well.

There were to be rough days ahead, and when they did return, if they returned, they would all never be the same again.

The corridor was narrow and stretched on and on, winding, rising, then dropping. Lord Merm followed behind his Captain. The rest of the Troop were in the rear. They carried large torches. Merm would take no chances. He had not gotten this far without learning to take simple precautionary moves. He had deciphered the second warning, but it was too vague and displayed no immediate threat to entering the passage. So he had proceeded with entry. He would return his attention, for now, to the discovery of the Key.

The corridor was eerie. There was the sound of running water and a fresh moist breeze within it. As Merm and his Troop made their way, the passage began to narrow. Its bare solid walls, smooth and old, rubbed their shoulders. Occasionally a cussing was heard from some Trooper that had bumped or hurt his head. They must continue on stooped. Whoever this passage had been built for was short and thin.

Merm's attention became distracted. His mind was being drawn to the coming days. He anticipated little resistance to his Troops after the Key was under his control. He had ordered all his armies to begin the move southward to test any resistance. By tomorrow the pathways around the Forest and Lake would be controlled again by the Gotts.

A darkness would follow in the sky wherever the Gotts traveled. It was the unannounced *evil* using the Lord as a pawn without his awareness. The third warning would tell of this, but in his rush Merm was sealing his own fate. The only ruling power in the end was to be the *evil* Magic of the Old Ones' enemy... Dorluc.

Dorluc lived in spirit form as long as there was Balance. As long as peace reined there was no fear of this master being resurrected. By hiding the Key and the *Passwords of Promise*, Dorluc could only try to win over the evil within us all and direct it subtly. But with the Key, he would be unleashed to terrorize and conquer. How foolish was this Merm and the Gotts!

Once before under Ho, Dorluc had almost managed to be freed. But Ho was limited in his abilities. Merm on the other hand, showed potential with his intellect as well as his greed. By the time the third warning was understood, Dorluc knew he would be able to manipulate Merm, just as he had manipulated many before on other worlds.

"Lord! The passage widens, and there is light ahead!"

The Captain rushed forward, Merm's attention returned to the corridor. "I can see…ah…!"

There was a splash, a gurgling noise, a horrifying scream and then silence.

"Captain…Captain…are you there? Captain?" Merm was concerned but more for his own welfare than the Captain's. How wise he had been to not take the lead. Merm called another Trooper forward to scout out the problem. The Trooper reluctantly went on. Very soon after he returned.

"Lord…a trap. The Captain is lost. A pit…full of water. There is only red water…No sign of the Captain."

"The second warning,…" mumbled Merm. They must proceed with care. He wondered at what the third warning foretold, but again that would have to wait. "Continue carefully. Onward."

As they approached the spot, it became clear what had occurred to the Captain. In his haste, the Captain had dropped his torch. Guided only by what seemed a dim light ahead, he had not noticed the correct path fork to the right, and so had continued forward to his demise. Clearly, care was a high priority now.

"Follow 'round. Careful," Merm announced. "Watch out for other tricks."

They all passed without further incidence. Within thirty lengths the passage way opened outward into a tremendous lighted cavern. Not surface light, but a yellow-green glow. It came from all over, on the walls and ceiling.

"My Lord…" commented Rmont…"It appears to be a plant. A plant that exudes light. A flower, but instead of scent, it gives light! What a marvelous find!"

"Yes, yes but we've come for the Key not a botany lesson. Look over there…"

About forty lengths beyond were two humongus

statues of two giant men seated upon large stone thrones. One had a lance in his right hand, the other a shield in his left. Above them was a roof like object, freely suspended. They towered so high, even the Gotts seemed insignificant in their presence. Between the two was another corridor and a tiny flat frame upon the cavern wall. Such extremes, noted Merm.

Whatever these GIANTS were guarding was clearly of great importance.

"It must be the hiding place of the Key. Let us stop a moment to gather our thoughts. Rmont, bring me the Fifth Book from my table in the castle. We will wait upon your return. Now be careful in the passageway. I DON'T want to lose the book!" Rmont bowed to the Lord and quickly retreated to fetch the book.

While they waited, the Troops settled in, marveling at the phenomenon of the luminescent plants. Even Lord Merm openly displayed intrigue.

"Lord," noticed a Trooper. "There's a writing in pictures on the base of the statues."

Merm approached to examine the find. Little rows of symbols followed by pictures covered the rock base. He had never viewed the like before. He ran his fingers over them as he thought, searching for some under-standing of their strange shapes.

"There is a story here of a magnificent race. The Old Ones truly had great power and magic." Merm was entranced, "I wonder at their purpose?"

What Merm failed to acknowledge was the reference in the Fifth Book of the *'Passwords of Promise'*, which were linked to the Key. These hieroglyphics were the instructions, as it were, for the complete and proper application of the calling of power that the Key would unlock. The *Passwords* revealed the secret of invincibility. Without their instruction, one could only tap into the power of *evil* or good that already existed within the controller of the Key. The balance between the two required great skill and teachings; neither of which Merm was acquainted. He was driven by power, greed, and of course... *evil*. Merm continued to examine the writings. He became very engrossed in their examination and lost himself to their mysteries. Before he knew it he was being interrupted by the voice of Rmont calling out to him:

"Lord... Lord... I am returned. I brought the book."

The out of breath Rmont was carrying the leather bound book. It was a little ragged, but it still contained much knowledge, limited only by the user.

Startled back to reality Merm motioned to Rmont and said:

"Bring it here, I will study it by the statues. Look what do you make of these?" Merm indicated the writings.

"Ummmmmmm," Rmont quickly made his way over to his Lord and stretched to read, touch, and otherwise dissect the 'pictures'. "Very interesting, perhaps these are messages, similar to the three warnings. Or maybe a history of the men who built these monuments. I really couldn't guess, Lord."

"Well let us look to the book for help."

The two sat at a makeshift table that one of the Troops had erected while Rmont and Merm were examining the pictures. They sat for a long time, arguing the nuances of this word or phrase from the book.

Finally, both agreed upon their latest translation of the second warning:

> ⁶Beware the Stoneman's long ago flight.
> He with the Key, hides in the fight.⁹

Both felt the reference was to the statues, written down long ago, when the Lord Ho had sought greatness and power.

"The Key must have been hidden here during the battles of the Separation War. Someone must have kept this Key from Ho and hidden it. That made sense, as Ho had lost at the crucial moment, with no good explanation. Somehow his power had weakened and he was unable to restore himself. It must have been the hiding of the Key!" Merm again exulted in his satisfactory explanation.

How wrong. Of course Ho had been beaten, but not as a result of a hiding of the Key, rather because he never found the Key. His strength came from the Magic of the *Passwords*, a magic which was too incomplete without the Key. But Ho knew nothing of these things. That was his downfall. For it was easy for the Old Ones and their guardians to re-establish the Balance with the true knowledge and power still hidden intact.

After several more moments of checking the book, Merm decided to proceed to search for the Key here in this cavern. He was drawn to and began to carefully investigate the alcove area beneath the statues. There was a small rectangular frame area on the far wall, but nothing else of note. He recalled reading of such a place in one of the Forbidden Books. Merm began to brighten. This must be the hiding place of the Key. Finally he would acquire the magic that would make him invincible. He motioned to Rmont to follow, then said:

"Let's see what is behind that tiny frame. I think it is the Key."

Merm went back between the statues, walked the ten lengths stopping directly in front of a little frame about waist level. It was no larger than a Gott hand. It was plain flat smooth. An insert was on the left side, similar to a book marker. He looked over his right shoulder. Rmont was eagerly waiting.

"Here we go!"

Merm pulled the tag and instantly a tiny door swung to the right, revealing a small niche which contained a golden box the size of a poorer Gott female's jewelry container. Silence surrounded the place. In a moment the container was in Merm's large palm. With his other hand he gingerly opened the marvelous container. There was a Key. It was very plain and made of brass. Grabbing hold he turned and showed the others, receiving shouts of joy and praise. The Key was his! The conquest could easily continue to advance as planned. No one could stop him now! Placing the Key back into its box, Merm turned and started back to the surface to the castle room. He beckoned Rmont to follow and to the others ordered:

"You five Troops remain to guard. The rest will return to their units and prepare. We ride with the second rising of the sun." then reducing his voice so that only Rmont could hear. "Have all my Commanders assembled in the main hall at midnight. I have some work to tend to."

They both left.

"I'm getting hungry Uncle Julian." Eruinn's stomach rumbled loudly, "We never ate breakfast and..."

"Stop complaining, we will soon rest. Remember we must hurry and find the entrance at the Lake of Choices," Princess Darla understood how, to the unseasoned, a journey of this type would be testing. She wanted to make the trip to the Lake without stopping for safety reasons and of course, to reach and stop Merm before he controlled the Key.

On their walk over the paths to the North they had begun to notice an absence of life. Everything was unusually quiet. It was strange. They did meet one or two travelers and each spoke of increasing numbers of strange Horsemen and now, the frequent Gott Troops. Had it already begun?

In another few hours they would reach the eastern hills and Lake, then on to the Lost Palace. They must continue and not waste precious time!

They had made better time than Darla's trip down. They had taken a more direct inland route, whose pathways were straight and not as winding as the more westerly ones. The pace had been grueling. Oddly there was not a peep from Julian or Thiunn, who were keeping up without problem. Darla's conundrum was, what the reaction would be, if one or the other youngster failed in the test of deservedness at the Lake. She shrugged off the horrible thought. It would have to be left to fate. That was all there was, nothing could change the providence of the Chosen.

The party was presently a little further northeast than Colleg's tavern. Avoidance was necessary. Prevention being better than cure. Darla hadn't relished the idea of bumping into the Riders again, and Colleg's place this far north must have been occasioned by both they and Gott Troops. Avoidance was the answer. In doing so however, it meant that their hunger and thirst would remain unsatisfied awhile longer.

They continued, and as they walked Eruinn began to sing a Jardian folk song:

> *"Up the Hill together we will go,*
> *Friendship and loved ones all.*
> *The pathways are long,*
> *But as long as there's song,*
> *Nothing can stand in the way."*

It was a silly song with many silly verses. Oddly enough, it did make one feel better!

"You wenchy know! Where go?!" demanded a frustrated Gorg of the innkeeper.

Gorg and Blag had arrived at Colleg's several hours before, supped and conversed with the innkeeper. When the mention of the female came up, Colleg told them she had been there just one night before. He didn't know her name and wasn't sure of her destination. Colleg's constant chatter and nonsensical ramble had caused Gorg's outburst, for Riders were not at all patient.

"Tell now!" in a threatening voice Gorg showed the white of his few remaining teeth, and tapped on the hilt of his sword.

"All you need do, is ask." replied a now nervous Colleg. "She was headed to the Summer Festival at Jard; wouldn't stay the night; was in the biggest hurry. She seemed afraid and hurt. She said she was going to sell medicinal herbs, but I didn't believe it. She was certainly on the run from something bad."

Tan smiled at Gorg. The innkeeper then understood that these two were the reason for the female's flight and desperation. Had he done right by telling so much. He was not certain, but he truly could not have lied. He knew what scoundrels like these and the Gott Troops would do just for fun, to get the truth out. He had a livelihood to watch after, and enemies had a habit of changing those things. Getting involved on any side would be counterproductive. He would be friendly to all, as long as they paid their tab!

Blag and Gorg huddled together to make their plans. They decided the best approach would be to send one Rider and one Trooper to Jard, under pretense of attending the Festival. Once there, they would seek out this female and quietly bring her here, where they would wait. It should take no longer than half a day there and back. No suspicion would be raised. In and out. They both picked their best corpsmen, ones that would draw the least attention, gave them their orders, and sent them on. After that was done, they called upon Colleg:

"Innkeeper. We will need rooms. See to it. We will enjoy our stay." announced Blag.

Colleg didn't appreciate his new guests. But money was money. He would play the Innkeeper routine and hope that they all left very soon.

He looked forward to a vacation after all this had passed.

Chapter 5.

B y the early eve the two outsiders rode into the
center of Jard. Though a few eyes were
momentarily diverted their way, not many
noticed. It was Summer Festival, a time of celebration
and acceptance. There were many different visitors
during this week of the season. In fact it was taken as a
compliment by most, that Jard was so famous in such a
variety of villages, and worlds.

The streets were filled with song and were so
crowded that it became a chore to cross them. Anyone
could be lost in moments amongst them. No matter
how large or smelly; the streets were a maze of citizens
and visitors.

The Village center was the main thoroughfare of the
southern route. Its pathway was made of gravel,
skirted on both sides by some of the finest shops and
merchants anywhere. It was commonly felt that if it
wasn't available in the Jard village center, it wasn't
worth having! All types of travelers passed this way,
and during the Festival, selection and choice became
unparalleled.

The buildings were mostly constructed of stone,
quarried nearby. Though Jard resembled a garden, it
had originally been barren and rocky. How beautifully
that had transformed with planning and decided effort.
There were no locks on the doors. No one need take,
when all was so freely offered. A very socially aware
village was this Jard; concerned about its citizens welfare and environment.

There was the smell of summer on the warm night

air, as Logue the Rider and his companion Flal of Gott, prepared to mingle with the crowd, in their search for the female.

"Now don't open your mouth! Let me do all the talking. We don't want to frighten these peaceful folk anymore than your smell already has." Flal had to put that jab in. "You keep an eye out for her, and I'll ask around, we're bound to find out something soon."

"Fine. I looky. You speak." were the only words Logue uttered. He disliked this Gott, but he was under orders to mind his actions till the wenchy had been found. He would get even later. See then how the Gott would beg for mercy. This vision humored Logue. The moment had passed on without reaction.

They started on the west side of the path, which was lined with some very large structures. They continued, going about two hundred lengths. All they found were just a few empty lots to the shanty town area, which was the place for all the Festival goers to make their camp for the week. Even this place was impeccably clean and tidy. Being in Jard had that effect on you.

There were incredible amounts of toys, crafts, and even food from all the regions being displayed in the many stalls. It was very distracting. Logue was to look for a familiar face, but Flal's plan was to seek out the herbalists and naturopathic medicines section. So far, he had encountered not even one. They went shop by shop, till they had reached the shanty area, where they both decided to stop for a beverage brewed especially in honor of the Festival.

A number of others were standing in small groups drinking and gossiping in the area. Flal made his way, paid for two tankards and returned to Logue who was pinned between three laughing and tipsy 'road lizards'. These were the women of the road who frequented a route, making their living. Not only was this a business trip to them, but also a treat…the Festival…lots of rewards!

Logue pushed away from them to grab one of the

tankards being offered to him by Flal, not noticing one Lizard holding her nose with thumb and finger making vile comments.

Logue and Flal moved closer together and sipped awhile, listening to the variety of conversations. There was all the local chat of acquaintances long parted inquiring into health, family, and business. Both Flal and Logue became disgusted with all the 'nice' intercourse. Finishing their draught, they left the crowded stand, crossed the path, and started back in the other direction. They only found more of the same type of stalls. About half way down, Flal asked of a vendor:

"Where are the herbal medicines?"

"Keep on going big fellow, you're just about there." he pointed down the path as he spoke.

"Good, now maybe we get somewhere, silly oaf!" Logue silently mumbled, shaking his head and at the same time rolling his eyes. He was frustrated and bored with the lack of speed in this pursuit. If only he could use his methods, then there would be results! On they walked.

Just ahead they came to another crowd, this time not at a refreshment stand, but in the section of naturopathies. The crowd was enthralled with the cure-all tonics and wondrous youth pills. It was very fascinating. Could they really grow hair on a ball? Flal and Logue, like the crowd, also found themselves captivated by all the claims of the remedies. But they had a mission to complete and could not remain to watch.

As they walked, their observance was drawn to one empty booth. Someone had not arrived at the Festival. Was it their female? Flal would feel out the neighboring stalls for any leads. This might be a lucky break!

"How unusual. I find it difficult to believe that the Festival is not a sell out. How come there are empty booths? Is Jard not doing well in these times? I know it has been a little rough. This surprises me and my friend here." Flal indicated Logue, who was standing to one side as he spoke loudly to the nearby vendors.

It had been too late to resell the booth for the first eve, and the Jardian organizers still expected their long time friend to show up. Maybe she had been delayed on the path? It would not be kind to give away this booth, until a fair wait was given. Certainly she would arrive by the morrow?

"No, no. That is 'D's booth. She has not yet arrived." answered the little dwarfish man whose booth was always beside 'D'. "With the trouble on the roads to the north she must have been delayed."

"Yes. It would not be the same without her. We have news to catch up on, and remedies to trade." commented another who was sitting with the dwarf.

"Not only that, she is such fun!" put in another.

"How so?" pursued Flal. This had been easier than he had expected. It was understandable though, since the area of Jard was open in all things. There was no need for secrets.

"Why I remember the time the Stoneman's son, Julian, bumped into her and made such a fuss. 'D' had us in tears with her description of the short, balding, husky little guy who was wobbling to and fro, not knowing what to say or do. He was more embarrassed than 'D'. He even tried to make up for his clumsiness by inviting her to tea. What a shy fellow. No one has ever seen him as fumbly!"

They all laughed, each retelling and recalling different versions of a tale told so many times that it hardly resembled the original occurrence.

Flal's attention perked up. This was it! Now we have her. Somehow he would have to pry the location of this Julian, from them, without raising suspicion. He thought a moment and when the laughter lulled added:

"This fellow sounds like a homeless poor soul. We see many in the North. They can be quite amusing in a pitiful way."

"On the contrary." responded one. "He is of one of the oldest families in Jard, with the most beautiful cottage and garden. It is just down that pathway at the second turn. What I wouldn't give to be in his 'homeless' condition!"

This seemed to ignite yet another round of joking and laughter. The Festival had all in the most jovial mood.

Flal looked at Logue. They nodded together showing a glint of a satisfactory smile. They would slowly move along and then recapture this female at her friend's cottage. She must have fled there for safety after her escape from the Riders that night.

The vendors continued the retelling of the stories and after a suitable time the Gott and the Rider moved along unnoticed towards the path, which they hoped would lead them to this 'D'.

Shortly the cottage appeared. Other than the lit outside porch lamp, no one seemed to be home. But it was too early even for a Jardian during Festival to have retired. After watching the entrance for a short time, they decided to move closer. The longer they stood around the more attention they would draw to themselves. They must be cautious.

Flal decided to approach and knock on the door. He knocked once. Then again. No answer. Seeing the side path he sent Logue to the back to find entry to the cottage. He knocked again...again. Then, there was answering at the door; Logue. He had broken a window in the back and crawled into the cottage.

"No body home is."

"Well look and see what you can find. Any indication that the female has been here." Flal ordered as he entered the cottage.

They searched using wooden matches for light. They did not want to light any of the cottage lamps since those would, by their brightness, attract unwanted attention from the neighboring cottages or passersby. Every now and then there was a muffled shout as a match burned someone's fingers.

As Logue searched he left a mess, throwing items all over. Making the mess made up for not finding any traces or clues in the Rider's mind. There were papers strewn everywhere, as if a tornado had struck.

Flal had given up and sat on the bed in one of the rooms. *'There must be something here to lead us.'* He thought.

As he lay thinking, Logue entered and swore at him to get back to helping him search. As they were about to continue the argument, between burning matches and fingers, Logue noticed the note that one of the youngsters had left behind. It had a paper weight upon it and lay on the bedside table.

"Ah...Looky what I find!"

He grabbed the note, but not being able to read, let alone speak; handed it to Flal:

> *'Dear Mother,*
>> *Do not worry we are all fine.*
> *Uncle Julian, 'D', my brother and myself*
> *must go north to Norkleau. All will be fine.*
> *We will return soon.*
>> *Must hurry.*
>>> *Love,*

He couldn't make out the name. But that didn't matter.

"So four there are!" echoed Logue.

"Yes four. It will slow her down and make it easier to track. Let us return to Colleg's and report." Flal was pleased, so was the Rider! They quickly left the cottage and made their way through Jard to find their rides and hurry back. They would reach Colleg's tavern by early morning. The mission was almost complete.

"After the next rise the Lake of Choices will be in view. We will rest there and have a corn biscuit."

All felt relief at the Princess's interruption of the song.

"How much longer till the entrance?" asked Eruinn.

"Not far at all. It is hidden at the base of the hill just before the water." it was Julian who had responded. Darla grinned.

"I see the prophesy is true. It does come back in time of need."

The outburst had shocked Julian more than anyone else. *How do I know this? I am just a Stoneman's son!*

Upon reaching the summit, the four stopped. What a magnificent view. You could see a great distance in unlimited directions. Straight ahead the Lake. The most azure blue imaginable. It reached forever exuding a serene majesty. One could make out the mountains of Gott caressing its eastern shore. The mountains rose rapidly in jagged succession till they touched the heavens, leaving white angel dust on the occasional peak. The shores below were wide and a fine whitish sand covered them undisturbed.

To the west was the Forest. The Burning Forest, so named, because of the constant fire that consumed one part or another, never being brought completely under control.

This was to be their starting point. How could something so naturally wonderful contain such terrors!

Thiunn noticed a darkness straight above, far over the Lake, hovering in place and pointed it out to Darla.

"That is Norkleau. The *evil* has started. We may already be too late."

The Princess knew now that the Key must almost be in the possession of Merm. The four must hurry to the Lost Palace to determine the amount of Magic the *evil* could wield. They were about to discover all the answers, even to questions not yet asked. But for now they must move on.

Working their way down the hillside, they found the path which lead to the eastern corner of the Lake. It was lined by wild shrubs. The shrubs were high enough to prevent a clear view, but Darla and Julian knew the way. It was just around the next turn. Just then, the noise of hoof-steps were heard over the sounds of the waves rolling onto the beach.

"Hold on. There are Horsemen ahead. Julian and Thiunn stay hidden, Eruinn and I will survey the path."

"We will wait till your return. Please be cautious," added Thiunn.

As Darla and Eruinn turned on the path out of view, Julian motioned Thiunn over behind a briar patch. They could sit on the large boulder which lay behind, well hidden and wait. They made their way over and sat side by side.

"Boy, Uncle Julian, this is quite a trip! I bet mother would be impressed. She never gave me any credit for being capable of doing anything so important. I never knew about Grand-dad. How is it that he became a protector of this Key?"

"I'm not so sure I know the whole story either," Julian thoughtfully began to answer. "It seems that our family came to Jard at its beginning, when it was only a desolate place. It was my understanding that we had come down from the north, as pioneers, or so I was always led to believe...People with an inquisitive and adventurous spirit, just trying to open the land and find a freer life, away from the conventions of a more stoic society. Instead it now turns out we were kind of fugitives, hiding not from the law but the *evil* forces of the worlds. It makes no sense. It would have been easy to find us here. Why were we left alone?"

"Maybe nobody realized who our forbears were. Who would consider a Stoneman to be a beholder of such gravity? After all, they spend their lives working with their hands, building homes and excavating rock. They didn't write books or make laws or even run villages. They were just hard workers. Maybe nobody suspected because they were too busy looking the other way for someone else. Someone in their mind more suited to such tasks."

"It does seem strange. Protector of the Key. Mere lowly me! To think of what is said about me in Jard, behind my back. I know I am ridiculed and made the center of many jokes."

"Well the joke is on them now. It's up to you and us to save their peace. They probably will never realize the role that we have played. Maybe that's just the way it is, in order to preserve against future threats. We are aces in a deck, even though we appear as the Jokers!"

They both laughed at the irony.

"What do you think this 'deservedness' test will be? Is it like a test at school?" Eruinn changed the subject.

"I don't know. You must be true and follow whatever inner instincts you may have at the time of testing, no matter what the end results may reveal themselves as being."

There was silence. It remained unbroken till:

"Julian! Eruinn!" came a whispered call.

Julian carefully peered through the briar. The others had returned.

"Behind the briar. Over here!" Julian called as Darla and Thiunn came over to them.

"There are Gott Troops all over, and many Horsemen, all heavily armed and ready for fight. Lord Merm has started his conquest of the Southland. They are presently encamped near our destination. It will be difficult to proceed in this light. We will need a plan, and cover of night." The Princess was noticeably concerned.

"But why invade the South. It is a peaceful place. What do the Gotts hope to gain?" asked Eruinn.

"Slaves and power. Not a good reason, but to the Gott, as good as any. Their leader, Lord Merm, is trying to rebuild the Empire of the Gott, similar to their last great tyrant, Lord Ho."

The youngsters instantly visualized all the tales of Ho, heard throughout Jardian childhood. This was an adequate explanation. What they hadn't picked up was the underlying force of *evil*; the *evil* of Dorluc, whose never ending quest to undermine the Balance was now gaining strength!

Dorluc had once lived in corporal form and was equal to and one of the Old Ones. During their quest for wisdom and knowledge, they uncovered the *Passwords of Promise* and the Key to invincibilities. The Old Ones were wise enough to see a Balance had been created to allow a certain freedom of choice in the manner of one's life. There was a desirable set of paths each could follow and improve upon, but not just one. This encouraged individualism and unshackled creative innovation. All were headed to the same end: pureness of spirit, and truth. From there the real journey, beyond the temptations of the flesh, could begin. It was the improving spirit that would give salvation, joy and peace. The resisting of temptation provided the test, so simple a design, yet, so terribly abused, neglected and missed by most. Simplicity always is the hardest route of attack.

When these truths were stumbled upon, the Old Ones decided to keep the mysteries secreted away. They would act as guardians, protecting the wisdom and Magic, allowing each generation to live in balance, making their own direction.

Initially there were some who disagreed with the decision. All except Dorluc had been convinced and eventually accepted the wisdom of the community. When it became clear that Dorluc would steal the knowledge and be so corrupted to the *evil* side of the Balance, the community banished him, never to return. The banishment did not hold long, for eventually Dorluc and some followers, manipulated and enticed by promises of wealth and power, were caught in an attempt to remove the Key and unlock the *Passwords of Promise*. This was clearly a violation of the guardianship and proof of the dangers of temptation. The Old Ones banished Dorluc and his group to the Land of No Form. He would be harmless there as an Old One. From there, his magic could only influence, not control.

Afterwards a second decision was made. The Old Ones decided to place into the hands of trusted souls, the Key. It would be the duty of these souls to abide the trust and conceal the Key, from even the Old Ones. Deep within these souls the knowledge would sleep, only awakened at time of need, returning dormant again after the need had passed. It was a wise arrangement, somewhat like temporarily forgetting a combination to a lock, but never losing it; a safeguard to a safe.

The Stonemen were respected honest craftsmen. They had a long history of integrity and loyalty of purpose. This integrity must have had a connection with the delicacy of their type of labor. Julian's progenitors had been leading masons of their day. So the duty came to rest upon his family. Because of the importance of double assurance, the obligation, once accepted for all generations of his seed, was deeply implanted into the soul of that distant forebear, locked even from his own conscious mind and quickly forgotten after the original performance of the task. It could never be coerced from the mind or body of its host. If by chance the Key was found, the current Stoneman's son would awaken, comprehend and act to execute the responsibilities entrusted to him, by the Old Ones.

Unlike Dorluc, the Old Ones eventually attained their pureness. They passed into the realm of spirit, giving up temporal existence for eternity, only having ethereal influence over the good, but not able to institute it.

They developed a system of guardians {Chosen Ones} who would have longer continuity and limited magic in order to combat disturbers of the Balance. These disturbers certainly would be predisposed to accept the *evil* counsel of Dorluc, from the Land of No Form. Julian would now have to deal with these circumstances and fulfill his destiny.

"If we are heedful, under cover of night we could pass their perimeter, find the entrance and continue on our way. The slightest sound or glimmer would give us away. Agreed?" Darla was convincing, and the others accepted her plan and analysis.

"Yes."

"Yes."

"Yes. Let's do it!" Julian and the youngsters were as ready as they could be.

It was fortunate that the sky had been darkened overhead by the *evil* of Dorluc. There would be no moon to give the four away. When it was dark, they quietly began.

When they were within earshot of the Troops voices, they squatted lower and leapt for cover from bush to bush.

The Troops were busy conversing over hot drinks, or play fighting, or just resting. They were nervous and uncertain as to what kind of resistance they would meet in the coming days.

Taking advantage of this, the four passed the distracted Troops, and came to an embankment. Julian told his nephews to be on the watch while he located the lever that would open the entrance to the secret passageway, allowing them to safely and in an undetected way move along to Norkleau. He again wondered at his new inner knowledge of these things.

"Now where is that lever?" Julian thought a moment.

The Princess also helped search. After several moments Thiunn warned:

"Uncle Julian, someone approaches. Hurry!"

Just as Julian found and pulled the lever, a Gott Trooper spotted Thiunn.

"Who's there? Stop! You little…"

"Quickly, everybody through the door!" cried out Julian so loud that the other Troops were now aware of their presence.

Eruinn, and Julian managed to rush inside, but Thiunn was trapped about fifteen lengths away. There

56

wasn't any time to plan. The Princess indicated that she would try to get the youngster, but the other two must go on. Julian was reluctant to leave. What should he do? Eruinn gave him a pleading glance.

"We can't leave them."

A cross arrow stopped short the conversation. The choice was made. The last vision Julian had, was one of Thiunn jumping between Darla and the path of a deadly cross arrow. There was a thud, and a cry. The door shut.

Not long after she had gone to bed, Lenore awoke from a bad dream. She had begun to feel anxious early in the evening after her two youngsters had failed to return home. She assumed they had stayed the night at their Uncle's, and would return home, the next morning. After all, they were growing up and as much as she worried about her brother's influence, it was definitely less harmful than strangers of the town! Still, some instinct was gnawing at her. She tried to ignore the sensation. She smiled to herself, realizing she was just probably missing those two. Since her widowhood four years ago, she hadn't relished the thought of the day when she would not have them around causing aggravation. Who would make her feel safe and needed, then?

Lenore was the only sibling Julian had. They were both very close as children and young adults, but after her marriage Julian felt that Lenore had changed, not dramatically, just enough to irritate. In her new found happiness and completion, she set about to marry off her brother. How could he bare to be so alone? He needed her help whether welcomed or not!

After several years of introductions and attempts which had all failed, Lenore's attitude changed yet again, to a mixture of jealousy and patronizing spite. Julian could not make head nor tail of the changes. Gradually he drifted more into seclusion from his family, not being able to tolerate the judgmentalism. The only villager needing judging was, in Julian's opinion, Lenore. Why do some females get on these missions, and when the conversion isn't successful their needy lost soul becomes a sacrificial lamb?! He had learnt to ignore her, and waited for the next change. Hopefully this one would return his old sister, the one with whom he so loved to share joys and tribulations.

Still half asleep in her bed, Lenore began gasping. It was as if a knife had pierced her right shoulder.

"Thiunn!" she called out. "Thiunn, my child. What has happened?"

She got out of her bed and pulling on her gown and slippers, decided that she must go to Julian's, *now*!

In half the normal time it would usually take, Lenore was outside knocking on Julian's front door.

"Very odd?" She noticed as she neared the cottage, "Why is the porch light on so late? If there's been drinking I'll finish that no good brother!"

Even as she threatened, somehow she knew something was very wrong. Inside her heart there was an apprehension.

"Julian? Thiunn…Eruinn!?" nervously calling out, partly because of the time and partly from her worry.

When no answer ensued, her panic began to swell. She tried the door knob, of course it wasn't locked! Entering, she tripped over the clutter in the hallway.

"Messy old goat," she muttered.

Finding a lamp inside, she lit it. As the light grew, she realized from the dishevelment, that all was not correct in her eccentric brother's universe. Even he was not that unkempt in home or being!

Making her way from room to room it dawned on her that a struggle must have taken place. Where were they? What had happened? She was used to the practical jokes Julian occasionally unleashed, but this was more.

Collapsing on the green leather sofa, tears filled her

eyes: "My sons! My family! What has become of them?" she sobbed.

As she wept, a ray of hope lifted her spirits. "Maybe the neighbors had heard something?" She immediately left the cottage and crossed over to Julian's nosiest neighbor. Standing weeping and desperate, she pounded upon the door:

"Help me, please H E L P...M E! Someone answer! Help!"

A light came on in the upper part of the home. Out through the window peered Andof Reed.

"Hey, what's going on! Don't you realize the time! You crazy Festival fool. Get lost!"

"Andof...It's me, Lenore. Julian is kidnapped and my sons disappeared. There has been a terrible fight. I fear for their lives!"

With that the window shut, and the front door opened. Mrs. Reed threw open her arms to capture the fainting Lenore.

"Andof, fetch the doctor, and then the authorities. It's Lenore all right, and in a frightening state!"

The doctor was still wearing his night shirt as he knocked on the Reeds' door, without Andof, who had gone on to fetch the authorities. He had been so rushed by Andof's urgency, that he had picked up his black bag and threw the first coat he found over himself to stop the chill of the night air, and any embarrassment for being out in his bedclothes. A shaken Mrs. Reed greeted him at the door and led him to Lenore. Lenore was in an hysterical condition. The doctor tended to her and as no amount of word soothed her condition, he reluctantly administered a strong sedative. As the drug was absorbed, Lenore began to calm down instantly, and timidly fought as the medicine pulled her to a deep peaceful sleep.

"I don't like to give this drug, but I've never seen such a frenzy. She will be okay. The drug will keep her asleep for a good day. I will return to check on her then. Does anyone know the cause of all this?" The doctor raised his eyebrows in anticipation of an interesting answer.

"No. None whatsoever. Andof has gone to fetch the authorities. Lenore mentioned something about a kidnapping or some such thing. We will have to wait till they explore the cottage of Julian next door. I am not going anywhere near till I know what's up!"

Mrs. Reed was a busybody, but only from a distance. She was not about to risk having her usually intruding nose cut off by some lurking fiend over at Julian's. She always thought he was a bit odd. After all, single at his age!

The doctor said his good nights, closed his bag and readjusting his coat to conceal his dress, left for home, where he would try to continue his interrupted sleep.

Andof's reappearance followed soon after the doctor had left. He brought the authorities in tow. He had been rapidly explaining the situation on the way. They decided to deposit Andof at his door before investigating. Andof would then have a chance to calm down and be safe. More importantly, he would be out of their way!

"Now Andof, remain inside and don't come out, and keep away from the windows. We will come back after our look-see."

The Sergeant in charge, was a middle aged individual who previously had served as a corporal in the Jardian Guard. Before he went over to Julian's, he left an officer in front of Andof's, taking the remaining two with him as backup, in case there was need of force.

As they entered Julian's they were shocked. Not only was there a mess, but the stench was choking. The Sergeant knew the aroma well.

"This is the work of the Gott, and Riders of the far Ice Barrens. I wonder what brought them so far from their limits. This is a violation not only of this cottage,

but also the Separation Tre~
this. There is trouble brewing. ~n't like the look of

The Sergeant was speaking ~
nates as they progressed in their of his subordi-
nothing other than the mess and sten~tigation, but
ing. When it became clear that there was forthcom-
that could be done, the Sergeant dismisse~hing more
walked back over to the Reeds'. Andof c~men and
meet him on the path. He didn't want his w~out to
was already upset, to overhear whatever the S~who
reported.   ~geant

"Not to be concerned. Whoever did this is long gone.
They won't be back. I'll send patrols around a bit more
over the next little while, if that's okay with you?"

"Oh yes please, {catching himself so as to appear
brave}. It would make the little wife feel safer. Thank
you, Sergeant."

"No trouble at all. It's all part of my job. I'll want to
ask a few questions of Lenore, when it's convenient?"

"Mrs. Reed said the doctor gave her a strong tran-
quilizer, and would be out for a good day."

"Fine, I'll come back. Good night Andof, and thanks
for coming to get us."

They shook hands, which was Jard custom. As the
Sergeant walked away, he made a note to report this
occurrence to the Jardian Guard in the morning. Just in
case this wasn't to prove to be an isolated happening.

While he made his way back down the pathway, the
Sergeant reminisced of the last time he had seen or
smelt the far north people. It had been during the time
he was in the Guard on maneuvers to the north in the
Burning Forest. A stray Troop of Gott, with a Rider as
guide {what a joke, he remembered} had encountered
his unit. Before these northern inhabitants were forced
back to their limits, three of his men had been mangled
and were dead. Not much was ever made of the event.
The politicians down played the occurrence in order to
continue the sense of a successful returning peace. A
peace that everyone then and now seemed to prioritize

The FLIGHT of preparation War, he had
in the Southlands. After another similar occur-
never expected to especially this far south. But why
rence in his lifetimosly. The hour was late and his
disturb himself through. He would deal with this
shift was just he wanted to return to the station and
tomorrow. As his second wedding anniversary, and
punch out ant to keep his home fire burning any
he didn't necessary.

Two years, how the time had flown. He was happy.
His wife was expecting their first child. He hoped this
evening's event was an anomaly. He didn't cherish the
notion of bringing a new life into a world that might be
on the brink of a horrendous struggle. He wanted his
son to be amongst the first of many generations born in
peace, never knowing or involved in war, famine or
destruction. The Sergeant had chosen well to raise his
family in Jard, or at least, he believed he had.

Flal raced Logue all the way back to Colleg's, each
wanting to be the first to tell the good news of their
discovery. By the time they were at the tavern, the
dawn had started to break over the eastern horizon. It
pierced through the pine tree tops, casting long thin
shadows and melting the dew on the sweet grass, in
strips.

Logue had arrived first. He jumped from his horse,
neglecting to tie it and hurried to the tavern door. It
was bolted. There hadn't been a bolt invented that
could prevent an excited Rider from passing. With a
crack the bolt and door gave way causing such a
clamor, that everyone awoke, thinking they were being
attacked! Gorg was the first to venture forth from his
room. He wasn't going to be caught with his pants
down, like a Gott Trooper might!

"Gorg. News I have of wenchy!"

"What! That you, idiot make such loud noise! What
news of wenchy?"

"Wenchy back North come, Norkleau. Maybe there already? Travel with three other now, she does. I find note!" He proudly displayed the crumpled note so that all present could have no doubt as to his story nor the splendid accomplishment of the task. This all left the impression that Flal was a laggard and of little assistance in the mission. Now Logue would really get even.

"So wenchy herself will capture. Will do our work. Comes back again. Merm will pleased be. All in two days only! Done Logue well. Proud leader I am."

Logue was beaming as Flal finally came into the tavern out of breath.

"Lieutenant..." Flal announced to the now present Blag.

"Yes, I heard." Blag was not pleased that the Rider had been the first to report.

"It should be easy to find her now, sir!" Flal tried to ease Blag's mood.

Merm had emphatically impressed upon the Lieutenant, before he met with the Riders that day, to not let Gorg and his Riders succeed. He wanted to teach the Riders a lesson and avoid payment. If Gorg produced results first, how could the Great Lord Merm deny the reward without tremendous loss of face? What a predicament. Blag found himself cornered. He was far from delighted with this turn of events.

"Flal, get some food and drink, then come to my room for a complete report. I want to know every last detail. Do not miss a thing." Blag hurried Flal away, then turning to his cohort suggested: "Gorg, after the debriefing I would suggest we mount up and head for Norkleau. I will send a messenger ahead to inform the Lord Merm of our good fortune and immediate return."

"We be ready," gloated Gorg.

Two Troopers held the now struggling Princess,

while Thiunn lay on the leafy damp ground in extraordinary pain. Darla had been saved the fate of the cross arrow, which, she felt, would with certainty have killed.

This had been a test of deservedness. Thiunn, by placing his need, second to that of another, had proven his pureness of purpose. It was over. Thiunn now started upon the path as not only a young Jardian, but also a Chosen One. Over the next while he would acquire the inner knowledge and the first magic.

The Magic came in stages. Darla thought back to her own initiation. Slowly she became capable of more. Her health was stronger and stamina longer lasting.

One of her initial abilities was that of the power of moving objects. At first, only small things budged, but soon, as she grew in the Chosen Magic, any thing could be moved.

Her power of manipulation improved. She found, in certain cases, slight suggestions could be placed in another's mind. It was a fascinating experience; one that continued to grow and develop. Even to this night she was learning more and more!

"My son! What have your brainless fools done to him! We are but peaceful travelers on the way to Jard!" acted the Princess. Thiunn, though in pain, realized what she was doing and would play along.

"Oh...mother I am hurt...ohhh the pain."

"It is but a scratch. Stop complaining little turd!" scolded one of the Troopers who was leaning over and examining Thiunn's wound.

It may have been a scratch to a nine foot Trooper, but to a four foot youngster, a cross arrow through the shoulder was a major injury!

"Get him on his feet! We will take them to Citol," one of the Troopers ordered.

Citol was their Troop Commander. He had been in the service all his life and had been passed over many times for promotion. He was at his zenith. How he had wished to become an aide attached to the Lord's garrison. But all this was academic now, at least that was how Citol thought. He sat alone in his quarters thinking on the *'could of beens'*. Little did he know how events were about to change. Now, shortly after the discovery of the two strangers, a Trooper stood in front of Citol's tent announcing:

"Commander, I have captured some spies. They are here for your inspection."

There would be no mention by this Trooper, of the other two who had mysteriously vanished into thin air. If Citol discovered this truth, all involved would be disgraced, stripped of their rank and pension. No one who saw the others, need be cajoled into keeping this secret. It was done as a matter of policy. Make a mistake as a Trooper and you were gone. Keep it concealed and you might get promoted. What a crazy infra structure these Gott lived by!

"Spies? Come." Citol ordered them enter. With the commencement of the conquest, everyone was quite paranoid about from where or by whom any resistance might originate. It was unfathomable that the South could be caught so unaware!

They all ducked as they entered and crossed through the flap door of Citol's tent.

"What's this? A youngster and a female! Spies?" he chuckled. The two least respectful items in the Gott society: females and children. They were both largely ignored and abused. It was laughable to even consider the possibility that the South had resorted to such low levels for support!

"Kind sir, my child and I are on the way to the Festival at Jard. We are not spies: My husband waits upon us there. We have lost our guide and our way." pleaded Darla, who broke free of the Troopers, to their embarrassment and ran to her weakening child.

"This is a nuisance. Why are you out so late?"

"We were afraid to camp the night along the path. There have been so may disappearances."

"I see." Citol glanced at his men, wondering if this

female realized in whose company she was. He decided to be careful. He wouldn't let them go free as yet. Even if they were not spies, they were to certainly cause an alert in the South if their story of capture were to be told. The Gotts would then lose any element of surprise. He decided to detain them, as guests here, till he decided what to do. They would not break camp for at least two dinners.

"Madam, I am sorry if we have inconvenienced you. We will care for the child and keep you as our guests."

"But sir, my husband will worry."

"Only for a short time. Do not distress yourself. These paths are dangerous. As soon as I can, I will send Troops along with you to provide safe passage. For now, accept my hospitality and apology. You will understand, my Troops also fear the uncertainties of these strange times in the North. In fact we are here to apprehend the culprits." Citol lied well. He would have been an asset to the Lord.

The Princess accepted the compromise graciously, understanding that this would give the youngster a chance to recover, and Julian a chance to complete his mission. They would be safe here amongst the enemy for a short time.

"Thank you, sir. That will make my husband grateful. Do you have medicines here, so that I might tend my son?"

Citol ordered one of the Troops to escort the two guests to the doctor.

"I bid you good night, Ma'am. Please let me know if there is anything that you need."

"Thank you again, sir." She left the tent with her son and a Trooper. She would need a plan soon. This Commander was hiding something. Perhaps he knew their true identity. She must use the advantage that she now held.

After Darla and Thiunn had left, Citol turned to his remaining Troopers.

"Where did you find those two, and what were they

doing here?" Citol could now get to the bottom of this without the female and child there to overhear.

"Sir, we were talking and relaxing, when a noise alerted Tooumas. He went to see, and we all heard a shout." replied one Trooper.

"Continue Tooumas," ordered Citol.

"Yes. It was as Vezat tells sir. I went to see what the noise was. I thought perhaps it was venison. A nice treat for the others. I silently crept up and there were two figures hiding just off the path in the bushes. I called out. There was no answer. I wasn't certain what it was. I still imagined it was a wild beast. Just as I was about to kill one, the other jumped forth stopping my shot from its kill. I ran to the fallen form and there was the child."

"Yes sir, we also heard a loud shouting and were drawn to the bushes where we caught the female," added two other Troopers.

"I see. But who made the shouting noise, you or them? Neither Vezat or Tooumas mentioned anything about shouting beyond the first calling out?"

One Trooper was quick to add:

"Yes...that's what we meant, sir. We heard Tooumas call out and came to see if he needed our help."

"Very well. Good effort everyone. They may not be spies, but it is odd to find Southlanders this far to the North. Keep a watch on them, but give them the free-dom of the camp limits. I will sleep on all of this in-formation. Make yourselves available in the morning, should I have further inquiries to make. Dismissed."

The Troopers with clenched fist over forehead, saluted their Commander and exited the tent. Citol was again left to his thoughts.

"So we have a female and child wandering the North. I will send word this night to the Garrison Commander in Aug, {which was the Gott Capital} in-form and request any intelligence pertaining to this type of business of wanderers in the North."

This incident might turn into an opportunity. The Garrison Commander in Aug would check all files and report back to Citol. If it was just an unrelated incidence, he would be impressed by Citol's rapid assessment of the potentialities of its handling and be certain to acknowledge his abilities and loyalties to the cause. This could find its way up the ladder and might even prompt a reward, such as a promotion. During these demanding times, High Command would be keeping an eye out for promising new blood which could better serve in a more powerful office.

Another possibility, could be that these were spies, whereupon the Garrison Commander would definitely draw to his superiors attention this quick wittedness of a before unnoticed Troop Commander in the field. Again leading to notice and reward of promotion. Citol could see no bad outcome whatsoever in his scenarios, other than the option to not report and take the chance of making a mistake.

Citol had climbed through the ranks from that of ordinary Trooper. He had no wealth and was generally respected by his line Troops. This had caused a great deal of envy and jealousy amongst his contemporaries in High Command. He was well aware of this fact, but did not allow it to disturb his skill as a Field Commander. It was only his natural command ability, that had kept at bay the upper echelons from trying to break him 'by the book'. He knew the book better than they. In fact, those others were much more susceptible to disciplinary action than Citol and were cognizant of this dilemma. It enraged their jealousy more. Nothing could be done. So Citol was left alone. This was about to change. With this capturing on the eve of conquest, even the High Command would not risk failure based upon personal likes and such.

Citol sat at his makeshift desk after dismissing the last Trooper. He quickly wrote a report and enclosed it in a plain white envelop. He sealed the envelop using the red wax and signet sealing ring of his lowly family.

He was pleased with the passage of events. In many ways he was thankful towards the female and child. Their discovery would act as a catalyst to his mundane career. How unpredictably one's life can change directions. Just when you think there is no more, a new door opens and on you pass to the new adventurous challenge!

What a time to be alive and a Gott!

Chapter 6.

Eruinn and Julian stood silently in the dark, not comprehending all that had so instantly passed. Everything had been over before they knew what was happening. The thought of Darla and Thiunn captured and maybe hurt by the Gott on the other side, was not pleasant. There was no going back. The door was closed and they were in the relative safety of a dark place.

"Uncle Julian, will we see them alive again?"

"Sure we will. That princess has many tricks up her sleeve, and your brother would drive anyone out of their mind till he was freed." Julian decided not to reveal what he had witnessed before the secret passage entrance had closed.

"We'd better get back to our journey. I don't know what information the Gotts will extricate from Darla or Thiunn. We will have to proceed with haste and caution, lest we are expected at the other end of this tunnel."

Julian made the effort to remove the worry of those left behind. He would do what he could after dealing with the issue of the Key. He wanted to believe that Darla would manage on her own, survive and meet up with them later.

These were the risks they had all accepted at the beginning. Events that seemed make believe, were currently hitting the mark with vivid realism and finality.

Eruinn interrupted his Uncle's thoughts:

"Where are we? We need a light. I brought the small kerosene lamp just in case. There's enough fuel to last several hours."

"Very helpful. I didn't think to bring a lamp. This will speed us to the Lost Palace." Julian's mind was back on track.

Eruinn undid his bag and pulled out a small orange lamp. He then took the lit half burned match from his Uncle's fingers, lifted the glass cover, turned up the wick and presto...light!

The lamplight revealed a marvelous entrance way. Its walls and ceiling were carved with ornate pictures. Every now and again script was below one. It was a language unknown to either of them, though it felt familiar. The pictures were telling a story and despite the sandy gray sameness of the rock carving, the pictures were full of life and color. In each, there was a symbol at the bottom right corner...****...curiously devoid of meaning.

Looking farther along, it was now clear that there was a path that went off to the right and beyond was a dark round opening. Julian took the lamp and started toward the opening.

"Eruinn, over this way. That dark area is the direction we travel. Come."

As they walked a yellowish circle of light was thrown by the lantern all around. Long shadows were propelled at differing angles, as Julian's motion swayed the lantern. It was spooky, and very very silent. It was so quiet that they could hear the crunching of the sandy soil under the weight of their boots.

Reaching the round darkened area, the lamp light stretched on. It revealed a corridor or tunnel. It seemed to be long.

"Is this the way Uncle Julian? I don't mind saying that all this is kind of bizarre."

"I know what you mean, but this is the only way to go."

On they went.

The corridor ran a slight downward grade, twisted left once and then continued level. The decor was as plain. There was no end in sight. They kept walking.

And walking. After what felt a very long time, Julian stopped.

"Let's rest and have some of those corn biscuits," he suggested. "We have made good time. Maybe we should try to get our bearings now, if we are able."

There was no disagreement from the youngster. Placing the lamp on the flat floor they sat down sharing the biscuits. Both were silent. Though many uncertainties ran through their minds, they refused to show it.

Shortly they rose and pressed onward. The corridor went on and soon narrowed. It began to climb at an incredible rate, causing the two to get out of breath by the effort of the hike.

"This is like going on a roller coaster," Eruinn was getting tired.

"It won't last long. Don't give up," encouraged his Uncle.

Just as rapidly as the passageway had climbed and narrowed, it abruptly ended. They found themselves inside a cavernous room, containing similar ornateness as the room of their entrance to this passageway by the lake.

"Let's spend a moment and try to make some sense of these pictures. There might be a good reason for them to appear again down here. Do you have any thoughts on what it might all mean? 'Cause I'm bewildered, myself. Look, each has the markings and each shows a picture of people dressed and doing things. What do you think?" Julian was perplexed

"Maybe they are all preparing something. A party or celebration or burial."

"Or more accurately a hiding! These tell of the hiding of the Magic! Look, the symbol there."

"Oh, yes, it could be. I don't get it. Why hide something only to advertise what it is that you're doing?" Eruinn noted in disbelief.

"Yes, it does seem counterproductive. Maybe there's more."

They continued to examine the pictures. Eventually frustration and the worry of what lay behind and ahead, forced them to quit and to resume their journey.

On the other side of this cavern was another darkened tunnel. Again they entered to find much the same sort of climbs and falls and turns as before.

Ten times a cavernous room appeared, identical to the previous ones. Ten times the tunnels continued. What was it all about? They had given up, for the moment, trying to understand more. They were extremely worn and not sure of anything anymore.

The sameness of their journey was broken as gradually the sound of water echoed throughout their current tunnel. Like the sound you hear when holding a sea shell to your ear. The lantern was still burning strong, but for how much longer? The tunnel began to widen to another cavernous opening. This time a big plain room containing two possible exits, not counting the entrance they entered from.

A dilemma arose. Should they split up and each take a path, or remain united on one? Which one? How to choose? They sat down on the floor to take the weight off their feet and think. They were tired. They looked to each other in hope of some help or explanation.

"What now?" Julian finally broke through the silence. "I never expected this eventuality. This was meant to be straight forward. What would Darla do?"

Eruinn had no answer. But they were going to have to pick.

"Perhaps the paths are only one, and rejoin each other down a bit further." Eruinn was thinking out loud. "Possibly one is a dead end, or there are two locations of hiding?"

Julian considered the choices. Splitting up was out of the question. If anything happened to the youngster, his sister would never forgive him, especially if this was the only one to return. Julian had never enjoyed making decisions. He did not have much practice at it, at all.

"My feeling, as this is a magical power, is to follow the *right* course. The right has always been representa- tive of good and protection. You know: 'Dieu et mon droit'. There could be a similar connection here. I may be completely off, but it does make a kind of sense. I suppose if we could understand the picture's meaning, we would really be more self assured now, but that is- n't an option."

"Your guess is better than mine. If your intuition feels the right is the better choice, then I agree and say let's go. We can always turn back if we encounter ob- vious direction changes. I just hope we don't have to go through this ten times more!"

"All right let's go!" Julian feigned self assurance. "To the Lost Palace!"

- - - - - - - - - - - - - - - - -

Time loses all meaning when you are encased in a world where the only transition or marker of the cycles of life, is a lamp. How long they were in the passage- way was unknown. Had it been a few hours or half a day or more? Disorientation had begun to set in upon them. Coupled with their progressing exhaustion, Julian and Eruinn were having problems orienting.

The water sound had become a cool underground river that trailed along with their pathway and was further complicating their minds. Whoever thought of a river, such as this, below the surface? But there was more. As it flowed along with them, it seemed to soothe, its gurgling reminiscent of a lulling chant.

Eruinn had gone as far as his young body could be forced. Mesmerized by the rush of the water, and the exhaustion of events, he finally collapsed.

"You must rest here awhile. We have both pushed ourselves beyond the limits. I am proud of you," Julian said. He also felt the strain of this journey.

Though the youngster was too tired to respond, Julian, using their bags as pillows, placed Eruinn in a comfortable position, turned the lantern off and with him, drifted into a well deserved nap. They had been on the move without sleep since the night before. In the

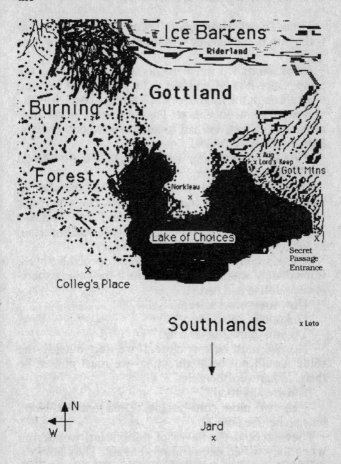

Map of the Northlands-- The Secret Passage Entrance

outside world, dawn had risen moments ago, but in their underground world, it was still one perpetual night. They had almost covered the distance of their journey north. The two cave travelers were nearing a destination. They must not sleep long!

Time passed. Eventually they awakened. It was before noon in the outside world of light. Here, still dark night.

Julian stretched out both his arms feeling for the lamp. Once he had grabbed it, he pulled it closer and went through the routine of the lighting. There was the yellowish glow once more. His eyes drank in the illumination so fast, he had to squint. He gently shook Eruinn into wakefulness.

"Eruinn we have slept long enough. It is time to go on. Wake up youngster."

Even as Julian said 'youngster', he had the realization that this was no longer the case. The youngster had now grown through the experiences of the last two nights {if that was correct, since Julian was uncertain as to the passage of time in the darkness}.

Eruinn's body twitched and then he opened his eyes, immediately squinting, having much the same experience as Julian had earlier.

"How long was I asleep?"

"Unknown. I also slept."

"Do you think it is far now?"

"No. We must be very close. If we were outside, the route would not be as direct, so we must almost be there. Wherever 'there' is!"

"Is there any food?"

"Yes, two more corn biscuits. Then that's it. Here, let's share one now."

They savored the flavor of the biscuit, wondering when they would eat a full meal again. They both recalled the Sunday dinner's Eruinn's mother made, with potatoes, pheasant, turnip, gravy and of course dessert! Eruinn had never been fond of the turnip, but now he would gladly have seconds even thirds, if it was offered!

It was time to move. Without speaking they rose and went on together.

Much of the earlier sameness of the tunnel passage continued. They had walked on and after awhile noticed a quieting of the river that had kept them company. It slowed and ended. It didn't just stop, it suddenly pooled into a small pond and that was all. There must have been an underwater outlet, for the rate of the traveling water hadn't slowed within the pool. There was a chill in the corridor, causing the two to have goose bumps. The lantern was starting to wane. On they went for a few hundred lengths and without warning, the passage, which had been level for the longest time, turned sharply to incline.

It wasn't long before Julian and Eruinn were climbing a steep grade on hand and foot. It was most difficult carrying the gear and lamp. Both hoped this was a sign of returning to the surface, and nearing the Lost Palace.

After what seemed a thousand paces, both stood upon a plateau. It had been a long haul. The air was musty and the surfaces around them made them feel cool. Both had hoped that after all this an end would be near. The endless monotony was wearing to them. They remained still, both recuperating from the climb and looking, as far as the light permitted for some sign of an ending to this underground passageway. They couldn't believe that they weren't near to it! To their astonishment there was yet another stairway which lay ahead. Again it was carved out of the rock. They were unable to see how far up it went for it was too dark. They would have to climb up. There was no other choice! They could not go back. They must go forward!

After the first steps the lamp extinguished itself. There was no more fuel. The darkness was unremittingly solid. Thank goodness there were still a few of the wooden matches left.

"Eruinn, grab onto my bag. We will save the

matches and as long as the stairwell lasts. We can slowly make our way up through the dark. It should be fine. We only need worry if the stairs stop or fork into different directions."

"No problem. That lamp light was getting to me anyway." Eruinn added this touch of humor.

Up they literally crawled, like infants on all fours. This went on for another three or four hundred steps, when Eruinn noticed, or thought he noticed, a glimmer of light.

"Look. Up there to the right. Is there a narrow beam of light? There! Do you see it? Just to the right ... ahead, about seventy lengths." Eruinn tried showing Julian.

Though it was too dark to see each other, Julian felt Eruinn's finger pointed toward the suspected glow. He strained his eyes, blinked, even rubbed them to be certain of their working clarity, and, yes, there it was, a very narrow sliver of a beam of white light.

"Yes, I see something, but it is very tiny. We must be near the surface. Strange though, I thought the Lost Palace was below the surface. Have we taken the wrong branch of the passageway?"

Then, half speaking to himself to try and bolster his courage.

"Well, there is only one way to discover. Let's keep climbing toward the light. We will soon know where we are."

"Oh thank goodness you see it too. I wasn't sure if my mind was beginning to play tricks on me. You know how it can be, like thirsty travelers on the hot sand lands. I never believed it could happen, but now I can see how easily desperate wishes can make your mind changeable to the point of unreliability. After a while, you can't be certain to trust what you think you hear or see!"

Citol, had earlier directed the messenger to bring a

reply, and to break all speed records in getting to and returning from Aug. He wanted the assurance of a reply by dawn. The trip had been swift and now the messenger stood waiting back outside of his Commander's tent, with the response.

"Enter." came a fitful voice, a little raspier than usual. Citol was coming down with a cold. This camping out, as he viewed it, was tough.

The messenger complied, and standing to attention, clicked his black boots together as he handed the response over to his Commander.

"Stand easy Trooper."

The letter was sealed. On the front embossed in the black wax of Gott, was the clear mark of the Aug Garrison Commander:

For Eyes only of: Com. Citol

It was hand written in black ink. Citol returned to his desk area, sat down, and breaking the seal read:

> *Commander Citol,*
> *Female of great interest to us here. Make arrangements to personally bring both captives to us at the Lord's Keep IMMEDIATLEY!*
> *It is of the highest priority that secrecy be maintained. You have done well to advise us so promptly.*
> *The Lord Merm certainly will be pleased.*
> *Make haste !*
> *Signed,*
> *Ruel, Commanding. AUG*

"Excellent! Trooper return to your unit, and thank you."

This type of gratitude wasn't necessary, but occasionally Citol used it to remind the Troops of his re-

79

spect for them, even though they were simply doing their duty. It made him a popular, though not always liked, Field Commander. As the messenger left, Citol added:

"Have four horses prepared for the trip to Aug, and tell the Unit Captain to meet me at the tent of our 'guests'. Also, send the Sub Commander to report here to me on the double!"

"Yes sir!" The Trooper fled out the flap door. Outside he met Sub Commander Tosh, who happened to be on his way to check on the watch. The Trooper conveyed the message. Tosh decided that the watch could wait.

"So, there is more to this. To react this quickly..." Tosh thought to himself as he approached Citol's tent.

"Uh uhmm," Tosh made noise from outside the tent flap door. "Sub Commander Tosh reporting as ordered, sir!"

" Enter." came Citol's reply. As Tosh entered Citol continued: "You will be in charge for a day or so. I have orders to report to Aug with our guests. Keep me up to date by messenger. If there are to be any changes I will send word. Any questions?"

"No sir. Things will be in good hands." Tosh was a little bewildered by the hurry of his Commander.

"Right then, Tosh. You have the reigns, Goodnight."

"Now sir?"

"Is there a problem?" Citol was preparing to leave.

"No, not at all. I just thought...

"Well don't. You are in command commencing *now*, until my return." Citol began to leave and added: "I expect to find this unit as I left it."

"Yes sir." Tosh saluted as Citol left for the tent of the two guests. He stood bewildered.

Outside the confinement tent the Unit Captain was waiting as ordered. He was a Gott in his twenties, who was still a little unseasoned, but had lots of promise. He reminded Citol of himself at that age and point in his career.

"Good evening Captain."

"Sir."

"You will accompany myself and our guests to the Garrison Commander at Lord's Keep. Apparently there is interest at the HIGHEST level in our innocents. I have ordered horses. See that they are brought here. We ride for Aug in moments."

"Yes sir, I will see right to it." he sped away

Citol then entered the tent of his 'guests'. Lying on the bed was the youngster. A camp medic was tending to his wound. The female was hovering nearby with an intent eye. She was nervous for the safety of Thiunn. The wound would heal fine, but the risk of infection and fever was still a likelihood.

"I will give him something to prevent infection, and control any fever," informed the medic, "but he should be kept still for a day or so."

Neither had noticed Citol standing at the entrance.

"I'm afraid that will not be a choice. Your presence is requested at the Lord's Keep. Wrap the youngster well, we leave now."

The medic obeyed without protest. After all it was only a Southlander child and female.

"Commander, I must protest. What right have…" she was cut off.

"My right is my sword, Madam. You *will* come and without further comment, or I shall bind and gag you. I have my orders, and you have yours. Now, let's not make this difficult." Citol menacingly smiled.

"But, why? For what purpose do you kidnap an innocent female with her child on the pathways? My husband…"

"Enough with this charade. Madam you are a prisoner of war and know far more than you would have us believe. It has been a good try. The game is up. My orders are to turn you over to the Garrison Commander in Aug. It is no longer in my hands. If you wish to complain, I suggest you do so at noon tomorrow, when we arrive. I don't for a moment believe your tale. Neither do my superiors."

"War? What war is this? These lands have been at peace…"

"The war that we are about to commence against your homelands. I have said too much. Madam bring the child. Now!"

It was at the mention of sword and war that Darla noticed she no longer had her jeweled sword! A panic set in, while she quickly retraced the events of the last hours from their capture to the present. She ascertained that it must have fallen during their surprise and capture. It must still be by the secret passage entrance!

In a way, losing her sword had helped the story of her son and herself, for Citol, even though talking with such bravado, still wasn't aware with what he was dealing. The sword would have created a totally different situation, one that might have resulted in much harsher treatment for Darla and Thiunn. She would show suitable protest to keep the Gott off guard, yet accept the current change. There would still be time to make plans, as long as they both were viewed to be of some unknown value. Besides, this maneuver would distract the *evil* from Julian and Eruinn. Perhaps they would still get to the Key before the Lord Merm, and stop the evil.

"Very well Commander, but you will regret this brutal treatment of us, and I formally protest, for the record!"

"So noted Ma'am."

They were escorted out of the tent. Darla held Thiunn, and carefully placed him on his horse. She mounted her's and the Unit Captain tied both their hands to their horses' pommels.

"Is this necessary?" Darla demanded of the Trooper.

"Standard procedure Ma'am. I have my orders."

Citol who had overheard and ignored the conversation rode off at the lead. The Unit Captain rode behind…just in case of an attempt to escape.

Thiunn found it difficult to ride, but realizing the need, managed. The medicine was helping a little. Darla privately hoped that it would be enough to see him through.

Just before noon, the trip through the mountain pass was over and the four horses paused on a vista rest area to behold the great Gott capital of Aug. It was a frightening, ominous sight with its dark spirals, and the Lord's Keep overshadowing all.

Aug derived its name from the month in which it had been created. It was the main center of any culture or intellect, {which wasn't much} and also the central Garrison for the militaristic society of the Gott. It was dirty, dingy, ugly, and threatening. There weren't enough words to describe its awful appearance and air.

The Lord's Keep was on the southwestern ridge. The only access to its main drawbridge, which was flanked by two very Gott-ish beasts peering down from their pedestals, was through the main path of Aug.

The Keep had been built by the first Gott leaders as part of a high mountain refuge, sharing on three sides a cliff drop of a thousand lengths to a torrid river below. Each subsequent Lord added to its construction, till finally it achieved an imposing and devilish majesty. It felt and looked cold, dark and evil. It was impregnable from a strategic perspective. Once within its walls or dungeons, the only departure was with the permission of the Lord. And that was usually after the party was dead. Even the residents of Aug preferred to remain on the outside and at a distance, having heard all the rumors of the dread that occurred within!

Citol noticed the look of religious 'fear' on his prisoners' faces.

"Ah, I see you have noticed our spectacle. The city of Aug, and the Lord's Keep. Enjoy the last few outside moments left to you. I don't believe you will leave from behind the walls of the Keep," he gave out a laugh, pleased that these two were certainly his ticket out of the field and into higher command. How he loved this place! Citol rode ahead, which increased the pace for the others to catch up, as they moved on and down the pathway taking them to Aug.

As they came to and rode through the city, Gotts yelled out rude comments aimed at the Southlanders. A rotten egg or tomato struck both Thiunn and Darla. This was part of the typical brutality of the Gott. The Field Commander sat erect in his mount with a grin that could only be compared to a contented cat after it had devoured its prey. By the time they arrived at the Keep's gates, the crowds had diminished.

A Gatekeeper called out for orders. Citol passed on his rank and purpose verbally. The drawbridge was lowered with a screeching and rumbling. They would be permitted to enter. The Garrison Commander was anxiously expecting them. A trumpet blew out to announce their arrival.

The moment for which Citol had waited, was rapidly approaching. What a change of tides to be welcomed a hero by the same comrades who had so openly disapproved of him before this day. Citol wondered what ever could surpass this achievement! He could hardly wait to see the look on Ruel's face!

Julian reached the top of the stairway first, and pulling Eruinn after, stopped an arms length away from the source of the light. Though there was a narrow beam of light shining, it was not wide enough to completely illuminate the surrounding area.

"Eruinn, give me a match."

"We only have two left."

"That's all right, I just need one, to see what is here."

Julian took the match and striking it against the rock staircase, lit it. The light revealed a door with one picture upon it and the... ****... symbols. The picture was of a large creature and was carved deeply into the rock. It looked like a Gott. What did it all mean?

Julian leaned over to the shaft of light, which was coming through a peep sized hole in the door. Closing one eye he gazed carefully through. On the other side he saw a large room, with what looked like a throne. There were Gotts all over and there in the forefront...

"Eruinn," Julian whispered. "It's the Princess and your brother. Their hands are tied, and they are on their knees!"

———————————

Upon arrival at the Lord's Keep, Citol, Darla, Thiunn and the Unit Captain had been ushered into the main hall of the Keep. It was lit by dirty antique candelabrums. Everything, other than the throne, was constructed of dark granite. There were Troops lined up, forming a channel down the middle of the hall. They stood like statues. As Citol and his 'guests' walked, every step taken by the four, echoed throughout this vast chamber.

Darla had never seen the inside of the Lord's Keep and after one look, decided the Gotts could 'keep' it. She always managed to stay in good spirits, though inside she was trembling.

Thiunn, was hobbling along beside, still recovering from the wound and the ill effects of the trip. He was awe struck by the grandeur of such a cathedral-like edifice. His fear was for the moment subdued, replaced by wonderment. He had never traveled outside the limits of Jard. So much had transpired in such little time, more than an average Jardian could have dreamt in a lifetime!

Before they knew it, Darla and Thiunn had walked between the Troops finding themselves standing before the raised platform that supported the throne. Citol and his Unit Captain forced the still tied captives to their knees. It was the proper etiquette for prisoners before the Garrison Commander!

They all waited in a long silence. Then a Trooper, from a door to the side and behind the throne, appeared.

"The Garrison Commander. Approach and be in fear!"

With that said, in came a large militarily garbed Gott, with two aides close at hand. He walked to the front of the throne, before the four visitors.

"Commander Citol, welcome. How good to see you."

The Garrison Commander turned without waiting for a response and approached the throne. This was Ruel. With an unsteady motion he sat awkwardly upon the oversized chair, facing Citol. Thiunn couldn't help but think it farcical. How diminuted this seemingly large Gott had become when seated upon the throne.

"So this is the female for whom the Lord Merm is searching? Who is the youngster?" Ruel continued to Citol.

"The female's son, Commander," came Citol's answer. Brief and confident.

"Please...please, Citol. We are equals and old friends. I am not only the Garrison Commander, address me by my name by all means!"

"Thank you sir...Ruel."

This was an unheard of break of protocol. Citol wondered at the importance of this female to cause such a stir?

"The Lord will be extremely generous for your capturing of these two. I feel certain a promotion will be in his mind as a reward. We may be seeing alot of each other in the near future."

"Nothing would please me more than to serve here with you sir...Ruel."

"I am sending word of our news. You don't mind me including my name?"

"By all means sir...Ruel. It would be an honor."

"To the Lord Merm encamped at Norkleau." Ruel dictated to one of his aides by his right side, "We will travel to you tomorrow with two guests that you will find interesting." It would be sent right away.

Ruel stood up and approached Darla. His two aides were still close.

"What is your name female?"

The Princess spat in his face. An outrage! If any other had committed such an insult, their head would have fallen to the floor. Instead he slapped her so hard, that she fell. One of his aides whispered into his right ear.

"Yes, I have a good thought. As the female is so brave, let us find out how she appreciates our best accommodation for prisoners of her class. Take them below!"

Two of the statue-like Troopers grabbed and dragged Darla and Thiunn off across the hall to the stairs on the northeastern side. Going below meant the filthy dungeons at the sub level. Disease and vermin made this hole their abode. The odor of rotten waste would make you ill, if the biting rats didn't!

"Put them together in a nicer cell. We must present them alive to the Lord!" Ruel shouted to the Troopers before they were out of view on the stairs.

"Yes sir." came an echoing acknowledgment.

"Everyone else is dismissed. Except you Citol."

The room cleared. Ruel advanced, put his arm around Citol and guided him out of the hall. They would celebrate over a festive repast.

———————————

The slap had startled Julian. He was outraged and bewildered. How had Darla and Thiunn arrived here at the Lost Palace? And why were so many Gotts here? And why was this place so lived in? And...Thiunn was alive! Thank the stars! While in his shock, he pulled back from the peep hole allowing Eruinn to see.

Eruinn watched as the two captives were dragged off and out of view of the peep hole. They were definitely in trouble. Julian and he would have to help.

"We have to do something and right away." Eruinn had a frightened tone to his voice. "But how do we pass this door and where will we find them?" wondered Julian out loud. "More importantly, where are we? If we are not in the Lost Palace, then where is the Key? You're right about one thing. We must rescue your brother and Darla, not only for their sake, but for the sake of us all! Darla will know where we are, and if it is not the Palace, then only she will be able to set us back upon the correct passageway. The hope of the South, is resting upon us all, together. Meanwhile, we had better discover the way past and returning through this portal. Once we manage to rescue your brother and Darla, we will require a quick and safe exit. I don't want to stay out there any longer than is essential to the job at hand. How many matches remain?"

"One."

"Then we must consider our next steps with the utmost care."

They sat in the dark for a few moments. Except for the sliver of light, they remained vacant of any other illumination.

Chapter 7.

At he bottom of the stairway, some forty lengths, was a series of short arched heavy wooden cell doors. Each was the height of a child. There was an opening through which food was shoved, whenever the guard could be bothered. There was also a ventilation, viewing space with two bars placed horizontally through its opening to prevent escape. A plate of food was occasionally permitted to pass, though it barely fit through. The stench of the place threw you over!

On the stone floor was browny-green straw thrown here and there to try and soak up the moisture which was seeping down the walls. The moat was above. The only way in or out of this hole, was past a sole Gott who was sitting on guard by the stairwell. He had full view of both cells and stairs. Darla hoped that there would be a chance of escape somewhere on the journey, from here in Aug to the Lord in Norkleau. It would be impossible to leave here without help and that didn't seem likely in the middle of a Gott stronghold.

A cell door right next to the seated Trooper lay open and waiting. Darla and Thiunn were dragged by the Troopers and in they were tossed, one after the other. They landed in the dark, wet, smelly hole. The straw was lying in clumps underneath them.

"Sweet dreams." along with obscenities were spoken by the two escorting Troopers as the door closed them in for the night.

It was a difficult adjustment for Thiunn and Darla to make, having never been forcibly confined in their lives; especially in this type of predicament. They anticipated a long wakeful night.

Beginning to notice more of the stench, Darla ripped both her shirt-sleeves and handed one to Thiunn.

"Wrap this over your nose. It will help."

Thiunn did as suggested. They both stood silently listening for the scurrying rats.

"Oh if only this were a bad dream." Thiunn pinched himself just in case. Ouch...no, they really were here!

Sitting in another dark room, Julian and Eruinn had been discussing their options. They tried to remember anything that would help.

"There has to be a way to open and close this door. I know we are not the first to come this way?" Julian was stumped. "Maybe there is some old knowledge within us that knows the answer? I feel like we should know what to do. There has to be a clue somewhere. Something that will unlock the knowledge and this door!" Julian fell silent for a few moments. Then Eruinn slowly began to express a thought:

"Remember what was chanted by Darla at your place? Wasn't there some mention of: a mason, that's you, two children, Thiunn and me, a woman, that's Darla, all know the tune. What does that last bit refer to? Maybe there's something musical in all this. Maybe some sort of musical combination will unlock this door?" Eruinn was thinking in the correct direction. His inner dormant awareness was revealing itself in small pieces. It prompted him on, "What do you think Uncle Julian?"

"Let's look for some indication to your theory on the door. Perhaps there will be something to help. Pass me that last match. I will light it. You look at the top portion of the pictures. I will look at the bottom portion. Commit as much to memory as you can while the light lasts. That will leave us only our memories in the dark, maybe there will be something, anything to help us along to rescue those two."

The match was struck.

"Look at those pictures, and there, the symbols again." Eruinn hurriedly reached out to touch one of the symbols and as he touched it, a note sounded, "That's interesting!"

"Try pushing them in order and see what happens. It seems your theory could be right." Julian was pleased with the discovery. Like Eruinn, it satisfied something that he didn't quite understand within himself.

"Okay." As Eruinn touched, each in its turn sounded a different note. "Notice any change, Uncle J?"

"No. Try different combinations."

The match was getting to its last holdable point.

"When the match goes out, we will have to continue in the dark. Remember where the symbols are." Eruinn acknowledged his Uncle.

They continued trying differing variations, even as the match flickered and went out, but still no result. Finally Julian spoke out of the darkness.

"Does it seem a coincidence that there are four symbols and four of us. Four that are involved: you, your brother, Darla, and me! Maybe we should press the four symbols together in unison. The four notes will sound a chord and may be the musical combination that will act as an unlocking mechanism? I'll take the two on the right and you take the remaining on the left. On the count of three we must push simultaneously."

Both, through the darkness, placed their hands lightly upon the symbols.

"Ready?" questioned the hidden Julian, who Eruinn could feel but not see next to him.

"All set."

"One...Two...Three!"

They pushed the symbols, and a chord...ray-fa-la-ti...sounded, followed by a metallic...CLICK. Something had unlocked!

"Here, let's try to lean against it and open it." Eruinn was excited at their apparent success.

As they leaned, the door began to open outwards.

"Here it goes!" strained Julian.

The door opened onto a stone balcony above the hall throne area. The sudden light temporarily blinded them. They crawled quietly out of the passageway, relieved to be free and back in the outside world, but at the same time afraid of what might now befall them in this *evil* place.

They found themselves on a tiny balcony that had a stairwell connecting it to the main hall below. It wasn't clear what the original purpose of such a small gallery was, but it probably acted as a place where an oratory could be given to a larger crowd listening below. Somewhat like the minister on Sunday giving a sermon from a pulpit.

They sat concealed, noticing that the hidden door would blend in perfectly with the granite stone wall once closed. No one would ever know of its existence.

"Well, now what?" Eruinn looked to Julian.

"We will have to go down into the hall, cross and go down the stairs there where you saw Darla and your brother taken. Hopefully we can do all this without being captured ourselves. Then all we have to do is rescue them. They must be in the dungeons below. There must also be guards. It is we two, unarmed, against uncertain odds. I don't see any other way."

It all seemed so improbable, so unrealistic. How could these two succeed? On the other hand, it was just because of this, that it might work. No Gott would have anticipated such a possibility from such an unlikely pair.

"What happens if we are seen, or heard?" Eruinn asked.

"As long as we leave this hidden passage door open, we can return, close the door, hide and try again later. I think though, there will only be one chance to rescue your brother and Darla. If we fail, the element of surprise will be gone and the guards more on the look-out. We will take it one step at a time: First, down the balcony stairs. Then across the hall. Then onto the stairs leading down. Find Darla and Thiunn, and finally get us all back here and through the door into relative safety. That's all. Simple."

Julian was being a bit sarcastic, but there were no other choices. The longer they waited, the greater the risk of discovery and failure. Now would be as good a time as any to begin.

"Well, I'll follow you Uncle Julian. We'll stop at the opening below the balcony." Eruinn indicated with his finger. "Do you think it wise to leave the passage door opened?"

"Yes. This place doesn't look very used anymore. It will be safe for the short amount of time that we will need. Anything else?"

"No. Just be careful."

"Don't worry. I plan on it. But you be careful too, your mother will kill me if something happens to you. Whatever goes on, the priority is getting us all safely out." Julian grasped Eruinn on the right shoulder. "We'd better go."

They crept to the balcony stairs and stood in a crouched manner. Step by step, one by one, they began to descend the spiral staircase. Within seconds, they were at the opening to the Great Hall. There didn't seem to be a guard on duty anywhere. Julian stood still while he checked the hall, trying to hide behind the corner wall opening upon the first step. He peeped carefully in every direction.

"Eruinn, I will go first. I'll go half way to the throne, hide and wait there. If the coast is clear, I'll wave for you to follow."

"Okay," came Eruinn's nervous reply. His heart was pounding and his lips were dry.

Julian gave one last look and then quickly darted the ten or so lengths across the open Hall to behind the throne. With every step he expected a guard who he had missed, to call out, or worse, a cross arrow to swoosh and thud into his body.

It seemed like an eternity, but he crossed effectively

in less than a few moments. He was safe, so far. He waited a moment, then, peeping from behind the throne, surveyed the rest of the hall. It was clear. He waved Eruinn to cross, and after much the same turmoil, Eruinn sat beside his Uncle upon the floor. Their hearts were still pounding as they were concealed behind the throne.

"Boy, that was scary. Are you ready to go on?" Julian was whispering between gasping for quiet breath.

"Yeah... but remind me to stay at home next time you ask... me ... for tea." Eruinn was perspiring.

"So let's try for the stairway across there. We will stop on the first step and try to keep hidden. Together... Ready?........Go!"

Julian led the way and again went through the nightmare of the crossing. Eruinn was right behind. They made it again, but now were in fairly open view. Should anyone enter the hall or come up the stairs, all would be lost.

They waited a moment to catch their breath, then started the slow trip down the stairs to the dungeons they hoped were below. After twenty-five or so steps the talking of the Cell Keeper and the two Troopers who had delivered the captives, became audible.

"Sounds like they're having a party down there." Eruinn noted.

Julian beckoned: "We will go more carefully and stop just as we get a viewpoint." Again he went first.

Shortly, the bottom of the stairs came into sight. What a mess. The floor was covered with a combination of fresh and old straw. The ensuing stench made it difficult for Julian and Eruinn to remain noiseless, but they did.

From their vantage point could be seen the lower bodies of the Troopers, a table with keys upon it, and a dish and a grungy bottle which, assumed Julian, had been half emptied by the three. There wasn't a way past them.

"What can we do Uncle J?"

"I don't know. It doesn't look easy and we're not in a position to spend lots of time thinking."

They both stood horrified as they considered their prospects. Then Eruinn who had placed a shaky hand into one of his pockets, found one lost match. How lucky it had not been discovered before.

"I know." he revealed the match as he spoke. "Fire. Let's start a fire and smoke them out. While they panic we can creep in under the smoke and do the job we came to do."

"Where did that come from?" But there was no time to worry over such things. Julian did not wait for Eruinn to answer, but continued: "How will we unlock their cells?"

"We grab those keys." Eruinn turned his head, guiding his Uncle with his stare to the table with the keys. "In the commotion, and pray to choose the correct one in time to open and then get out of there before we are discovered."

"How are we going to get the match lit and onto the straw without notice?" Julian whispered. He was not looking forward to the next move. He expected it was to be his duty!

"That's harder. I'll have to creep lower down, light the match, then throw it away from the opening and then get back here. When it starts up, it will spread fast. Then we move." Eruinn was right. They would have to move fast. That was all they could do.

Without challenging the plan, Julian nodded in agreement, as Eruinn began a careful descent. Julian realized that the youngster was smaller than he and could probably go longer unnoticed by the large Gotts below. It was their only real choice of action.

In fifteen steps Eruinn reached a good spot. He took scope of the situation. The Troopers were busy laughing and drinking. They were seated at the end of the table farthest from him, facing away from the direction of the cell stairs, that would help. He decided upon the best spot of straw he could see, lit the match and gently, as it ignited, threw it upon that spot. It began to smolder and then grew into a tiny flame. He carefully backed up to Julian.

"I think that will do it." Eruinn had taken great risk.

"Now." Julian took command. "When it gets going the Troopers will panic and try to put out the flames. You find their cells, while I get the keys. We will release Thiunn and Darla and then all of us return back the way you and I came, to the passageway door." Julian prayed it would continue smoothly.

It wasn't long before the smoldering heat of the match had started the spread of smoke from amongst the straw and was filling the room, so far unnoticed by the Troopers. It was not until it had burst into a large flame that one of the Troopers smelt something different, above the normal stench, and in turning, discovered the cause.

"Fire!"

The other two jumped up. All three proceeded to deal with the by now billowing smoke.

Now was the moment!

As the Troopers passed the stairway, Julian and Eruinn leapt into the dungeon area. Julian grabbed the keys from the table as quietly as he could and Eruinn ran from cell to cell in search of the captives, tapping upon the doors. They went unnoticed during the panic of fire and the concern of the Troopers about their punishment once the Garrison Commander discovered this clumsiness.

Darla and Thiunn, like the Gotts, had also been unaware of any rescue attempt, till Darla began to smell the smoke and hear the yell of the Troopers.

"Something is up," she alerted Thiunn. "Be prepared to move. This could be help."

With that they waited and listened. When the knock came at their door, they rushed to it and recognizing Eruinn through the barred opening, called:

"Eruinn over here!"

Eruinn hearing and then seeing the two through the thickening smoke, got Julian's attention to bring the keys so they could open the cell. Julian crossed to the cell door fumbling with the keys. He tried one, then another. Finally, the third key opened the lock. The captives pushed the heavy cell door outward, and by doing so, the noise drew the eyes of the Troopers.

"Follow us and don't stop!" Julian directed.

They all crossed over to the stairs through the choking smell of smoke and stench. Their eyes were watering from the dense smoke. Eruinn was in the lead.

At the same moment one Trooper, realizing the escape that was in progress and its ramifications on his own career, lunged after the four who were beginning to climb to the hall above. He just managed to grip onto one of the escapees.

Julian had been the last to step onto the stairs. He was trying to protect the others as they climbed.

"Eruinn!" came his startled voice.

A Gott Trooper had him by one arm and no matter how he twisted or squirmed he could not break free.

"Eruinn I'm caught! Save yourselves before it is too late!"

The other three hearing the call, stopped in their tracks. Eruinn grabbed a wooden wall torch and returned to aid his Uncle. This was twice now that he had risked his own safety, showing deservedness. Darla and Thiunn were close behind. As Eruinn arrived, he quickly understood the route to take. Without flinching, he yelled and struck the hairy Trooper repeatedly with the lit end of the torch. The large beast held its prey. Again Eruinn struck as Darla and Thiunn pulled. This time he pushed the flame into the Trooper's bearded face; it caught the hair on fire. The Trooper screamed in pain and let go just as his other Trooper comrades were coming to help. The freed Julian, pulled up by Thiunn and Darla, continued upward to the hall above.

At the top, in the Hall, they darted without care to-

wards the balcony stairs. The Troopers were in hot
pursuit and new ones were entering from the main
doors after hearing the alert from the cell keeper. They
must hurry; up the stairway and onto the balcony they
went! The Gott Troops were almost atop them, being
able to close the distance separating their prey faster
than the four expected. Gott strides were so much
longer!

There was no entrance! *IT HAD CLOSED!*

"But we left it open... right here! Now we're in a
mess!" Julian did not need this added problem.

"Don't worry Uncle Julian, all we need do is sing the
chord." Eruinn began to hum, "It's ray-fa-la-ti. Darla
hum ray and don't stop till we all are in unison,
Thiunn, fa."

Darla started off. There was no time to question
singing at a time like this. They just had to do what
was asked. "Uncle J, la and me..."

The four sang their note, holding it, till finally a four
note chord could be distinguished. The Troopers were
now on their way up the balcony stairs. Clink; the unlocking sound, but this time the stone door opened under its own power.

"Quick get in!" someone ordered and each scurried
through. "Help me pull it shut."

The four each grabbed any available part of the stone
door. Just as the Troopers turned the last step, it shut.

"Where'd they go?" was all the Troopers asked.
They had seen them go up the stairs and expected the
four to be trapped there. The concealment was perfect.

"Back down! They must have jumped below. Search
every corner. The Garrison Commander will not like
this. I had better report right away."

The Troopers descended, splitting up to more efficiently search the Hall. One lone Trooper would report. The rest felt relieved not to have to be the bearer
of such awful news.

Behind the passage door the four were catching their
breath. They were also glad to be safe from the reach

of the Gott Troopers.

"That was a close one." Darla was first to speak. "How did you know the pass-tune?"

"It's hard to explain. Before in that dark we seemed to become more in touch with our inner beings. Something inside each of us awakened. Eruinn had a feeling or a 'knowing', we tried and it worked. But where are we and how did you two get here? Is this the Lost Palace? What of the Key?" Julian fired questions at her.

"Slow down." exclaimed Darla. "This is the Lord's Keep in the Gott capital of Aug. Thiunn and I were brought here to the Garrison Commander."

"You mean that slob who slapped you?" commented Eruinn.

"Yes, but how did you know?" wondered Darla.

Eruinn explained briefly how both he and Julian had happened upon this door to the outside, being drawn by the light. He showed her the sole shaft of light and the peep hole. Darla peered through and then understood.

"We were to be taken tomorrow to Norkleau where Lord Merm is currently camped. But how did you manage to find 'this' route? I thought you two would both be in Norkleau by this point, and what of the Key?"

"I hope we still have time." panicked Thiunn.

"We somehow chose this path and it led us here. We weren't aware of the possibility of another secret pathway and destination. We were lost ourselves, when we happened upon this peep hole and spotted you two. We knew something was wrong and that we had to rescue you in order to find out where we were and how to get back on the right path to find Norkleau." Julian was a little aggravated by Darla's tone. He sensed that she was not impressed with his or Eruinn's inability to take the correct passageway. It didn't seem to matter that it was lucky that they hadn't, and, as a result, had been able to save she and Thiunn from their incarceration—a rescue that hadn't been given any acknowledgment or thanks. What about the Key and the Gotts? Was there still time to complete their task? He felt patronized.

"It was a good move, Julian." relented Darla. "I will put the three of you back onto the path to the Lost Palace, and then I must return to find my sword. I will catch up with you at Norkleau."

They continued chatting and answering each other's queries for a while, recounting all that had occurred since they had parted at the Lake of Choices. This finally satisfied Julian and made him feel more appreciated. He realized as they all spoke together in the darkness of the passage, that part of the problem was the stress of the dark, and another part was irritation at Darla's 'taking over' control without as much as a 'thank you' or 'do you mind'. Julian decided to ignore these feelings. It was obviously the extreme conditions that were making him more sensitive. They must continue getting along with each other if they were to be successful. They were a team.

After they had exhausted the stories, Darla suggested that they all rest for a short period, then continue the journey and their mission. She, or rather her inner awakenings, knew these passages well and there would be no problem in getting onto the correct path. All agreed. They stretched out and instantly slept.

———————————

The Sergeant eventually returned to the Reeds' home to ask Lenore a few questions. It was afternoon, two days later. He had been very troubled by the apparent invasion of Julian's home and subsequent kidnapping. All the details that were made available to him that night of Andof's call, had been reported the next day to the Jardian Guard. They were most interested in the event. Why would these Northlanders come so far south? Why bother a simple Jardian such as Julian, and his nephews? They felt that there must be more to it and encouraged the Sergeant to follow up the questioning whenever Lenore was capable. So here he stood, in front of the Reed's awaiting an answer to his knock.

"Good afternoon, Sergeant," Mrs. Reed opened the cottage front door.

"Good afternoon, Mrs. Reed. Might I ask Lenore a few questions with regard to the incident of the other night? My superiors would like the loose ends tied up as soon as I am able."

"Well, she is still quite shaken, but if you are delicate, I believe Lenore would not mind. Please come in and have a seat. Can I get you tea?"

"Why thank you, that would be fine."

"Good, I'll put on the pot and fetch Lenore. Please, make yourself at home." Mrs. Reed showed him into a lovely sitting room off the main entrance.

———

The Trooper stood, knocked, and announced himself outside the quarters of Commander Ruel. The Commander answered.

"Yes Trooper. Why do you disturb me at my dinner?" Ruel had been celebrating with Citol, acting very chummy. Both were pleased with their new outlooks on future and career.

"Sir....Ah...."

"Get on with it Trooper!"

"Sir... The prisoners have escaped." He bowed his head awaiting the rage that would follow.

"What! Are you responsible for this stupidity? No one has ever escaped the dungeons of the Lord's Keep!" Ruel was shouting at the unfortunate messenger.

Inside, the rest of the celebrating party became interested in the activity, stopping their revelry to listen. Citol was alarmed and rose.

"What's this? Escape! They can't be far, organize an immediate search!" Citol interjected.

"I will handle this if you don't mind, Commander." Ruel was returning to his old ways, but he was careful to appear outwardly calm amongst this audience. He did not wish his dinner guests to see his 'other' side so publicly. He must act the part as a firm fair and respected leader.

"You mean as you've handled my captives so far. This is unfathomable!" Citol was seeing all his hopes vanish. This turn of events might even set him back farther. He had to turn this around, and somehow save his position and responsibility in the eyes of Lord Merm. The Lord had been sent a messenger bringing good news. He would be furious when new word of this escape arrived, especially after having had his spirits lifted. Citol wanted Ruel's blame to be clear.

"Sir. We have searched and are continuing to search. They are not to be found. They had help from others. The cell keeper spoke of two others of same size starting a fire and releasing them. They all disappeared in the Great Hall." The Trooper was very nervous. "I came directly here to report, knowing the importance to the Commander."

"Yes you were wise. Return to the search. I will come directly. Dismissed." Ruel turned back to his room of dinner guests who were standing in silence. He kept control of his inner rage and animosity toward Citol. He would get even in other ways without alienating himself from the others.

Eruinn was the first to open his eyes. He half expected to be back in his own bed in Jard, but he wasn't. In the outside world it was late evening. He moved on his hands and knees in the darkness of the passage till he found another and awoke the body. "Who's that?"

"Thiunn."

Eruinn hugged his unaware brother.

"Oh dear Thiunn, how glad I am that you are well.

When we were separated I was so worried. I didn't know if we would see each other again."

"I wasn't sure I would see you again either. But here we are." They hugged again. There had been no time earlier for such relaxation.

The others were also beginning to stir. It was time to embark upon their mission. Darla pulled out a luminescent oblong object from her pocket. It irradiated just enough dim light to make out the others.

"This will help us see in here. It is an old device left to me by my parents. I have no idea how it works. But it does come in handy now and again. We must retrace your steps in here. The second fork in the pathway is under the river. Do not ask me how I know this, I just know. There is also a stirring within me just like you, and I am becoming aware of more as the need arises. All will be fine."

"Under the river? But we of Jard don't swim." there was a worried edge to Julian's voice. "I don't think I can learn now."

"You don't have to swim." The inner knowledge was becoming more clear. "You have to hold your breath longer than anyone thinks they can, sink down and the current will pull you through. Hopefully you will live to see the other side!"

It wasn't clear if Darla was pulling his leg or not. The two youngsters weren't very excited about the idea of water either.

"There is no other way. The need is strong. It must be done. It is a sort of protection against unwanted intruders to the Lost Palace. Going back to the first fork at the Lake is too far to travel. We must waste as little of this precious time that is left us, as possible. After I see you on your way, you will know what to do. Simply follow the passageway. It will take you to the Palace. I will catch up with you there. Do not wait or slow down on my account. Don't worry, anyone who can rescue and escape the dungeons of Lord's Keep, can survive the less dangerous, perils ahead."

"What if we lose our way again? Then what will we do?" Julian was not ready to be left without Darla again.

"You will have Thiunn and Eruinn to help you. I believe that they have both passed the test of deservedness and now will begin to be in tune with the powers of the Lost Palace. They will know what to do, should I be delayed. Now we should move."

With that, all four proceeded down the stone staircase, which was faster now that there was light. It would not take long to retrace their way to where the river had ended in a swirling pool. The thought of that deep colored water brought chills to all but Darla.

"If only there was a less suffocating alternative. The water…ugh…of all the means to dissuade…why water? Ugh…" each of the three were speechless, in their private apprehension.

"Good afternoon Sergeant." Lenore came into the sitting room.

"Good afternoon. I do not wish to inconvenience you, but I do have some questions." he stood as he began to talk, offering his physical guidance towards the thick cloth settee. As Lenore sat, Mrs. Reed brought the tea.

"Oh there you are Lenore. Will you have tea?"

She set the tray upon a little table and began to pour. As she poured, she handed a cup and saucer to each, including herself.

"If you don't mind Mrs. Reed, it would be more comfortable if Lenore and myself spoke after the tea in private. Please take no offense, it's the company's policy."

"Oh no problem, I still have some baking to tend to. You go right ahead, I'll go into the kitchen now."

"Thank you." He rose as Mrs. Reed left.

"Lenore, just two or three questions."

"I'm ready, but I don't know what I can offer to be

of help. The last time I saw Eruinn and Thiunn was before they left for tea with their Uncle..." She began to sob.

"I'm sorry if this is painful. I won't delay you long, but this could be of help."

"Yes. Please excuse me. I am so concerned."

"Did the youngsters mention anything about a trip perhaps?"

"No. It was just tea at Julian's. They were to be home before dark."

"What about this woman?"

"Woman?"

"Yes a naturopath from the North. She was meant to arrive for the Festival and hasn't appeared. She rented a booth. Some of her friends were worried and came to report to me yesterday. They suggested, perhaps she was with your brother?"

"No." Lenore became indignant. How dare Julian expose her two innocents to that *type* of woman. She would have words with him and then she remembered and weakened once more. "I never heard... any mention...of...{sniffling}...such a person..."

"It's probably unrelated. I'm just covering all the bases. Well, that's all I wanted to ask." he began to rise up as he spoke. "I won't keep you anymore. Thank you again. I will keep you informed of our progress. I'll see myself out. Good day." The Sergeant walked to the door, opened it, and left.

The echo of the messenger's walk up the stairs to deliver Ruel's speedy note, was loud. Norkleau Castle was smaller than Lord's Keep but still impressive, not in darkness but in bright magnificence. Lord Merm hated it. The Trooper reported to the Unit Commander, who in turn accompanied him to Rmont. Rmont opened and read the note.

"Excellent. The Lord will be pleased. You are dismissed. Refresh yourself and then return to the

Garrison Commander in Aug. Tell him we await his speediest arrival."

The Trooper saluted and withdrew.

Rmont proceeded to the secluded castle room where Merm had been working on the last warning since the midnight meeting.

The meeting of the commanders at midnight had gone as expected. The Lord had entered to salutes and clicking of boots. There were twelve, thirteen including the Lord. They had stood waiting till Merm bade them to relax.

"Gentlemen, please sit." Merm sat at the head of the large conference table. The commanders took their places.

"We are now ready to consider commencement of the preliminary expeditions into the South. There has been peace for a considerable time, and we need to verify the ability of our enemy to respond. I suggest sending the Seventh Division in as soon as they can be mobilized. Commander Frid, are your Troops ready?"

"Lord, my Troops are on the move at your command, this very night, if it is desired."

"See to it then. Keep us informed of your progress."

"At your command Lord," Frid rose, saluted, and bowing his head toward Merm, took his leave.

"The rest of you are to be on ready alert. Within two sun risings we will follow the conquest plan. Any talk?"

"Lord. What are we to do with prisoners?" a question was posed to which all wanted a response.

"Keep the ones who can provide service. The others I leave to your discretion."

The commanders were satisfied. Truly this was a great leader of the Gotts.

Hearing no other questions, Merm began to rise, signaling the conclusion of the meeting and causing the others to follow suit. "You have your orders. Good luck commanders."

Eleven thank-you's of acknowledgment were given.

The room cleared.

"So it begins!" Merm had long anticipated this time. It felt good. "I will finish the last warning and then get one last pleasant sleep. There will be no holding back the Gott Empire!"

He left the hall for his private chamber.

- - - - - - - - - - - - - - - - - -

By the very early hours of the pre dawn, Merm was exhausted. He still hadn't broken the last warning. The box with the Key sat in front of him on the table amongst the papers. There was a knock on the door.

"Yes... who bothers me?"

"Rmont...Lord. I bring a message delivered this moment from Aug."

Merm stirred. After a thoughtful pause...

"Well what are you waiting for? ENTER!"

Rmont passed through the door, came down the stairs, and stood before the arched window.

"My Lord." He offered the message. "They have captured the female and a youngster. The Garrison Commander feels she is the one for whom we search. He will bring them both today."

Merm excitedly grabbed the paper from Rmont's grasp.

"Who is the Commander in Aug?"

"Ruel. Apparently a Field Commander by the name of... Citol... made the initial capture earlier, near the Lake of Choices."

"This is working just fine. We have the Key, the first two warnings, and now the female. Perhaps she will help in the final deciphering of the last warning. Then we can go forward without any more apprehension, or delay. Send word of my pleasure to Commanders' Ruel and Citol. Tell them great reward awaits."

"My Lord it is already taken care of. The same Trooper returns now to Aug."

"This calls for a drink to celebrate. Rmont join me in a mug."

"Yes my Lord."
"I feel great things about to emerge!"

Back down the steep incline of the passageway, after the plateau, and on through the level tunnel, their return journey progressed. Soon the sound of the rushing river could be heard.

"There, we are almost at the pool." Eruinn's heart dropped. Soon they would be submerged in it!

On they hurried till...

"This is it all right." confirmed Darla. "See the central area where the whirlpool is?" She pointed with the illuminator, so the others could just make it out in the dim light. "That's where you go under, about forty lengths. Eventually you will surface in another pool on the other side of this wall. Just follow the river and the path."

The sound and rush of the deep water was far from inviting. The three stood fear-stricken, thinking of all the dreadful eventualities.

"JULIAN. Julian." Darla's voice snapped him out of the trance. "You go first. Wait on the other side."

Darla watched as Julian started testing the water, feet first. He looked at her.

"I don't think I can do this!" he shook his head and mumbled, "I can't swim. I can't do it!" He took his feet out of the water and stood firmly on the path.

"You must. There is no choice. It is your calling." Darla realized what she must say. "Don't let your father down. It is your time to act." She had approached him and placed her arms around him to comfort him. She had almost whispered the last sentence to give it more intimacy. "They," she indicated Eruinn and Thiunn, "need to see your strength. Go now!"

The 'go now' ran in his thought's, but it was not Darla's voice. It was that of another...It reminded him of his father. He pulled himself together and slowly walked into the river, immersing himself up to his waist. His feet were touching the river bed. It slanted at a sharp angle down toward the whirlpool causing him to be unstable in his stand. The pull of the river was powerful. It was now or never. Julian gave a glance then slid completely into the control of the river. Round in large circles he went his head bobbing up and down.

"Take the deepest breath you can...N O W !" shouted Darla. Her use of the 'voice' had worked and Julian was on his way.

In moments his husky body was sucked into the water. Nothing remained except a few bubbles of his short scream. Thiunn and Eruinn froze.

"Okay, you two go together. Hold hands, and don't forget to take a deep breath. Hold it till you feel like you're gonna burst. As soon as you pass through, pull yourselves to the surface. Even in the dark, you will know which way is up. Here, take the illuminator. Use it after you get back onto the path. I will be fine. I can use the sheath on my return to light the way. Good luck." She indicated the sheath on her side.

They grabbed each others' hand and stood frozen by the fear of the water. Darla waited.

"Go on." She was getting impatient. "Jump in!"

Still nothing. She leaned over to the two as they were watching the river, pushed and s p l a s h they were in and complaining.

"Take a deep breath, before it's too late!"

Up and down they bobbed like their Uncle and then they too were sucked below, into the watery depths.

"I've never seen such foolish fear of water." Darla spoke out loud though nobody was there to hear, "Good luck my friends."

She then turned and undid the strap which held the sheath of her missing sword to her side, and bringing it before her face began to concentrate upon it. Gradually the small gems that adorned it began to exude a faint light. It would be enough to guide her. She turned and then sped on towards her own destiny.

Chapter 8.

Merm was asleep. It had been one of his best days in a long while. How fortunate to have found the female. He would sleep well now. After Rmont had left, he drifted into a brief secure rest, his dreams vivid. He was the Lord of all lands, Conqueror. All bowed before him. The Key was hung and carried on a golden chain around his neck. The Key was all power. The Key was the glory. He must use the Key!

Dorluc was tampering with his unconscious thoughts, encouraging and persuading Merm to begin to use the Key. By displaying the images Merm wanted to see, and enhancing their strength of reality, Dorluc hoped to influence Merm into the rapid use of the powerful tool instead of waiting until the third warning was deciphered.

Power, glory, winnings, great wealth—all of these were displayed in Merm's dreaming mind. It was an amazingly simple feat to accomplish when the participant was eager and willing—like Merm!

This recurring dream had been implanted many times now. Since the beginning of Merm's rise to power, it had helped in his obsession for conquest. It made him feel self-confident in accomplishing his vision of a reestablished Gott Empire; moreover it continued to sway and lead him to the *evil* of Dorluc.

It was Dorluc who had helped Merm's knowledge of the old tongue, enabling him to discover the existence of the Key. He had also implanted deeper within Merm's subconscious, the idea of more power: the *Passwords of Promise*. Again, none of this had been particularly difficult to cultivate in a mind of one, such as the Lord Merm. So compulsive was his desire, that he hadn't even begun to suspect his being manipulated. By the time he realized, it would be too late and then Dorluc would be the complete master acting through Merm.

"What a fool these types are!" thought Dorluc. "So ignorant to the real influences, blinded by their own meaningless ambitions." Dorluc would enjoy his final actualization through Merm.

First on Dorluc's list, would be to rid the worlds of any Chosen Ones. Then he could reign unbridled for eternity. It would be a time of enslavement and misery for all others, a time of increased magic and better knowledge of the *evil* that lay waiting to be used. How silly of the Old Ones to avoid the Magic's immediate rewards and continue to struggle for all those years, till finally they had gone on. Gone on to what? Love? Peace? Knowledge? What pleasure was there in these? Dorluc became disgusted every time he thought of them. How fortunate he had been banished to the Land of the Formless. When he was finished with Merm, he would be able to sample all the lusts he still clamored after. He needed more, and more and more. The taste was insatiable. Lord Merm will make that all possible! He would continue to influence the dream sequences until the Magic was unveiled and he could live again.

There would be no 'Old Ones' left to challenge his rise to influence over the worlds, but he had one concern. Dorluc recently was becoming aware of shifts or changes within the Magic. He was not able to understand their meaning, but there was some difference in the power. A change that he hadn't felt since the Old Ones existed in the worlds.

He probed the mind of Merm to reveal whatever was known, but it was impossible to get beyond the haze of ambition and greed. He must keep a guarded eye himself on the changes and monitor their growth.

Meanwhile, Merm's dreams required attention.

Everything was so close. In a matter of a very short time, the conquesting Troopers would devour the South. The beginning of the doom. Once the Key was properly used, there would be unlimited magic. He must get Merm to use the Key. Use the Key. Use the Key! Why wasn't Merm responding? What was getting in the way of the suggestion? This was all part of the changes felt by Dorluc; he didn't like it. It was a thorn in his side—the wild card.

Merm was in ecstasy. The dreams were so real that he began to wonder if he was awake or asleep. He kept seeing the vision of success and power, but now the Key seemed to be linked to the success. He felt that he should pursue the magic that the Key contained. No, not yet, only after the third warning. He was struggling against a suggestion to forget the third warning and focus on the Key. Merm was still in control and the Key could wait. It was something important; he wanted to find out what the third message said. After all, Lord Ho may have made a similar error. He would not repeat the same mistakes. So it took a little longer, in the end, Merm knew his caution would pay off.

In his dream he could fantasize. In the real world, he must follow the required steps to preserve and protect what he knew was his providence. There was also this female to contend with.

Merm had discovered long ago the importance of a methodical approach. It had given him the leadership of the Gott. When others rushed, they tended to later get slowed down by the seemingly insignificant problems not taken care of at an earlier time. They rushed ahead, till the little things had grown into uncontrollable cancers. He would not be tempted into the same trap of so many before. Dorluc, although unknown to Merm at this instant, would not yet be able to over-ride Merm's strong will or sensibilities. Dorluc would have to wait, settling for the minor influence he had now.

"The moment will come." Dorluc thought in his formless home. "The moment will come!"

At the same time as Blag and Gorg were awaiting reports from Flal and Logue, the Gott Troops to the southwest received the order to begin the campaign to test the resistance and strength of any opposition. They were to be an advance group, small enough to combat any unpredicted force, large enough to hold the territory gained. They were to make sorties into the bordering villages and take control of the northern routes.

As is the Gott way, they began the first expedition in the dead of night. The division of Troopers and Horsemen had been stationed on the border long before. These Troops were the ones who had been responsible for all the recent unrest on the northern routes. They didn't understand the lack of apparent alarm in the South that these raids should have drawn. Was the South that unprepared? It seemed unbelievable that the South would disband an entire force after the Separation War? The facts spoke for themselves. No resistance or interest was yet aroused!

By the late dawn of this first sortie, Colleg's tavern had been reached. All the neighboring little communities of farmers had been easily captured, their thatched roof cottages set ablaze. No casualties were incurred by the Troopers, but several of the farmers had been killed, especially the old and young. If it hadn't been for the need of food and crops, all would have been destroyed.

The surprise attack had been a success, the progress very fast. Absolutely no resistance. Where were the Jardian Guard? This far north was their responsibility! At this pace, the Gotts would be in Jard within one more sunrise. But those were not the orders. This division was merely to secure the North. It was going well. Messengers would relay the news to the Lord at Norkleau.

The smell and sight of fire filled the skies. The dark of the *evil* was penetrating deeper.

Flal and Logue were still being privately debriefed, in their respective *commander's* rooms, when out of the morning dew entered yet another Gott and his entourage. Colleg had been wary ever since the visit of the first Troopers and Riders. But this early morn, entrance of this Seventh Division Commander to Colleg's home, was the icing on the cake; so many guests, one right behind the other!

"Innkeeper! Innkeeper make yourself known!" It was Frid.

Colleg appeared as usual. "Yes, good traveler, are you to breakfast this early dawn?" He once again played the part that had saved him numerous times before.

"I am Commander Frid of the Seventh Division Troop of the Gott. I hereby seize this place. You sir will be spared, as long as we have need of you. Get us food and drink, and be warned, do not interfere."

Colleg was petrified. It took all his energy to move without falling down in fright.

"Yes...sir ...Right away. My ...home is yours!" He ran off to the kitchen. Colleg instantly decided to send word to Jard by way of his pigeons that were kept in the back by the kitchen. He must warn of this invasion, while he still could. It wouldn't be noticed if he acted immediately.

Blag had been quickly informed of the arrival of the Division Commander. He abruptly stopped his debriefing and exited his room to go and introduce himself. He was on the second floor landing when he recognized the Commander:

"Commander Frid!" he called out in a friendly voice as Frid looked up.

"Lieutenant Blag!" Frid smiled. "What are you and these Riders doing here?"

Blag came down the stairs and each of the two shook hands and grunted familiarities. They were old acquaintances. They moved to a large table and sat. Each began to recount the experiences and news of the past while.

As this was going on in the main dining room, Colleg had been left alone in the back kitchen. He was scribbling a note. He attached it to one of his best birds, which he cuddled and spoke to gently, directing her to fly to Jard. He then quietly opened a rear window and watched as the bird flew high into the southern morning sky.

"Thank the heavens!" Colleg murmured. Nobody had noticed, in all the arriving hubbub.

This was to be Frid's headquarters. The realization made Colleg's knees buckle. He had to get a grip on himself, or he would not survive the occupation.

The Sergeant was busy talking to the Area Captain of the Jard Guard. They were reviewing all the facts of the disappearance of Julian. Both agreed that something was very wrong.

It was mid morning and a glorious day.

"No, I don't believe this is a prank, or that they have gone on a vacation forgetting to leave word. What about the mess inside the cottage?" the Sergeant was weary from the strain of thinking of explanations

"I agree, but why Julian? He is of no ransom value or anything else. The youngsters had no importance either. The suggestion of the involvement of this woman 'D', is just as ludicrous." The Captain was trying to make sense of it.

"Why come down from the North after these individuals? It is rare, even during Festival for Gotts to venture south. There has to be a good reason. What do these three or four have in common, that make it worth the northern tribes taking a risk by coming to Jard?"

The two had been bouncing ideas back and forth since the beginning of the day. Still nothing had arisen of substance. They both were tired.

"Let's get a warm drink and refresh ourselves."

The Captain got up and looked out the window and

gazed into the blue sky. He saw the clear air, the tops of green trees, and in the distance the foothills of the area to the North. There was also one lone flying object that appeared to be headed in this direction.

"What do you make of *that*?" He pointed out the object to the Sergeant? "Over there, straight ahead."

The Sergeant leaned out and stared in the direction of the pointed finger.

"Looks like a bird?" he said in a matter of fact way.

"No, not just a bird. A carrier bird. You can tell by it's directness of flight. It's going to come here."

They watched and waited till eventually the bird, a pigeon, flew above and landed on the ledge of the roof. Attached to it's leg was a small white piece of paper.

"We'd better get to the roof and check this out. Are you coming Sergeant?"

They ran to the stairs that would lead them to the roof. Once atop the building, they approached the edge. Looking over, they saw sitting on the ledge, the carrier bird.

"Lovely birdie. Come here, such a clever birdie." The Captain was cooing and making kissing sounds. The Sergeant was amazed that such a macho type could act this way. It was embarrassingly humorous.

"Well don't just stand there. Help! We need to get that message!" said the Captain, becoming irritated as he noticed the Sergeant's ridiculing glance.

The two kept praising and coaxing the creature, who many times came towards them and then just turned the other way. Finally, thinking the Captain was offering food, the bird came within reach. The Sergeant took hold in a caressing way, presenting the leg and the attached note to the Captain. They would see that the bird was cared for after they had read the note. The Captain removed and unfurled the tiny paper. The scribble made it difficult to read:

Send help! Gotts have invaded! Taken prisoners! Many will be killed. Using my Inn as

headquarters!
PROTECT YOURSELVES!   *Colleg.*

The Sergeant knew Colleg. During his tour in the
North there had been many a night spent at the tavern
drinking and just passing the slow moving time.

"I know this fellow. A good person though a little
seedy. If he writes of trouble it must be serious. He
was not one to send alarm on minor events."

"I don't like all these things happening at once. It
seems we might be under some sort of invasion. What
part does the other night have to play in all this?"

"I don't know, but I had better go and prepare my
men."

"Yes, I will inform the Area Chief. We must hurry.
If what this Colleg says is true, we have been caught
with our pants down. I'm not certain we can organize
this fast. Let's hope these invaders are satisfied awhile
and give us opportunity to arm!"

'D''s friends were still worried. The authorities had
been nice enough, but made it clear that especially at
this time of year every able body was busy. They were
short handed. They would do what they could, but it
wouldn't be till after the Summer Festival that much
more attention could be paid.

That might be too late! 'D''s friends feared for the
worst. There had been rumors of trouble to the North,
the disappearances and the talk of large amounts of
Gott Troopers becoming visible on the border. There
was an impending sense of doom for 'D' and themselves. So many strange things had been going on everywhere.

Still the village was celebrating as if there were to be
no tomorrow. This Festival had been touted the best in
years and it was. Never before had selection been so
varied, in attendees and their wares.

- - - - - - - - - - - - - - - - - -

The Jardians, after the Separation War, had disbanded most of their forces. They had also rid themselves of weapons, all as a gesture of good faith. How naive this generation had become. They believed that all races would want the same in life; respecting the weaker and stronger equally; never resorting to brutality, but rather discussion and debate. They were fools. That was Julian's opinion, and a few others.

It was so easy for the tolerant majority to write off the Julians of the worlds, as old, out of date, fanatical war mongers. Little did they know!

Julian had often wondered at the ability of intelligence to grab onto stupidity and dangerous thinking. The more dressed up or disguised it was, no matter how obvious in ulterior motives, the more readily it was accepted, with such proud self destructive fervor. However had they all survived? A little bit of wisdom surely was a dangerous thing. Fools did rush in where angels fear to travel. The old maxims held great truth.

It had been too frustrating for those like himself to bear. So they turned from the apparent majority, praying that their own existence would not be disturbed by this foolhardy ignorance, that was in the control of the future, for the moment.

The Sergeant made his way to the Mayor's in the building across the main street. He had already spoken with Area Chief Mal, briefly informing him of the crisis. He would meet him at the Mayor's.

As the Sergeant entered, the Area Chief was waiting in the outer room of the Mayor's office. The Mayor was still in a meeting with the local dignitaries. The door opened. There was laughter as the Mayor stepped out followed by his deputy. They noticed the waiting Jardians.

"Good afternoon Mal, Zer. How are you?" The Mayor offered his hand.

"Good afternoon Mayor, Deputy, sir," both replied

in turn.

"We were just going to lunch, can this wait?"

"I'm afraid not, sir. In fact, this will concern you all." There was a look of consternation on their faces.

"Could we go into your office, sir? It is rather urgent."

As Mal spoke, he indicated that the reason for his visit should not be overheard. He tilted his head in the direction of the others in the outer waiting room, so as not to draw any more of their inquisitiveness. The Mayor caught on.

"Let's talk about this in my office. Gentlemen?" They retreated behind and closed the door. The others, waiting or working in the outer room, paused a moment, shrugged, then continued unaffected. You know how the authorities like to feel their own importance!

"Sirs. There has been a report of invasion from the Gotts in the North!"

"What!" although all had been startled, the Major's voice was the loudest. It was heard even in the outer room.

"The Sergeant has informed me that a short while ago a carrier bird brought this message." He handed it to the Mayor and, in turn, on to the Deputy. They all sat down in despair.

"This is impossible! Why everyone agreed to stop such primitive behavior!" The Mayor could not believe this was happening.

Finally, the naive stupidity of the majority was striking its knoll. The Mayor silently and unconsciously, amongst other thoughts, realized the validity of the Julian group, {as he called them} that had protested on continued disarming. He had ignored them. They weren't politically popular, even though their vision was more correct! If this event proved to be corroborative, he was in trouble.

"Primitive or not, we must accept the potentialities and act accordingly." Mal continued.

"What are you suggesting, Mal? That we comply in

the same manner? Two wrongs won't make a right!" The Deputy was just as stupid as the others!

"Sirs, with all due respect, we have no option but to fend them off, or be treated in the same regard as the villagers already invaded by them. If we don't act, we will be overrun by the Gotts and the other mercenaries in their employ. Need I paint the picture of rape and pillage that we all know too well from the history of the Separation War?" Mal was tired of politicians. He was a man of fighting, not words. He knew what they potentially were about to deal with and the odds would not be in their favor! It may already be passed the time of stopping.

"But how is this possible?" the Deputy added.

"That's all academic now. The crux is that we are in the middle of a fighting situation. I recommend we mobilize at once."

This was a great moment for Mal. He would be in command and win great glory.

"Very well, but before we totally engage I want some corroboration on all this. Then, we'll decide."

The Mayor rose saying his good-byes. There were things to tend to if this was to be a fight.

Mal and Zer dismissed themselves. All had to prepare for what could develop into an inevitable bloody fight. The Deputy remained.

Sergeant Zer returned to his station, reported to his superiors, then decided to take one last look at Julian's cottage. Something was drawing him. He felt that there had to be a reason for the disappearances, and ramshackled rooms. There must be a clue. He hurriedly left the station.

Upon arriving at the cottage, he entered through the back, where he imagined the initial break-in had occurred. Carefully examining the tiniest markings, he made his way through the cottage. Again he rechecked drawers, cupboards, counters—nothing. He sat on the bureau chair looking nowhere in particular—pens, pad, letters, bills. There was a clue here, so simple, it had to have been overlooked. What could it be? He tried to imagine himself in some similar panic situation where there wasn't a chance to call for help. What would he do in the few short moments before being rushed, attacked, or threatened, if there had been a chance? He sat and stared and became trance like in his awareness.

He couldn't decide. His eyes went over the bureau again. Nothing. Pen on the right. Pad in center, letters, etc. He lay his head on the desk. Nothing. He lifted his head, ready to give up, when there it was! The pad. Something had been written on the page before, leaving an invisible impression on the next sheet below. Maybe it was just a grocery list?

He took a lead pencil and ever-so lightly shaded over the sheet where the impressions lay, word by word, till it could be clearly read:

> 'Dear Mother,
>   Do not worry we are all fine.
> Uncle Julian, 'D', my brother and myself
> must go north to Norkleau. All will be fine.
> We will return soon.
>   Must hurry.
>   Love,   Thiunn xoxx

This was the overlooked clue!

Suddenly it all began to make sense. Norkleau was in the Gottland. Were they captives or on some mission? No one in their right mind would travel on the northern paths, let alone go into Norkleau. He knew it was said that this 'D' was more than she let on, but why would the two youngsters go along. They would only slow them down, causing difficulty. No, they must have been taken by force, which could explain the mess here. But the note, it was too relaxed. Unless the youngster had been made to write the letter in order to delay any maternal fears and create unwanted alarm, which would draw attention to what was now building in the North! Yes, that had to be the explanation!

Zer was reasoning faster than he could think the words. Still, why had there been a need for these four? Or was it just the female and in order to keep all silent, all were taken along. Yes, it fits, what, I'm not sure, but it does provide a reasonable premise to start from. Zer's trained mind was rapidly building a scenario of the events of that night. If they were captives there would be little that could be done. The Gott would discredit any attempt to have blame laid upon them without hard proof. On top of that, if there was about to be a fight between North and South, then the only acknowledgment that could result was confirmation of the four as P.O.W's. They would still be imprisoned.

There was a greater issue here that Zer confronted. Maybe they were spies and this was merely a cover-up to camouflage their genuine purpose. The more he considered, the more the plot thickened.

He decided to leave his extrapolations aside. It was time to report and also inform Lenore of this new finding. At least it was clear that the 'kidnapped' youngsters were very likely alive and well. This would comfort alot of their mother's fears.

Zer was still mulling over everything as he left the front door heading next to the Reeds'. Lenore had decided to remain, so as to be close and in view of Julian's cottage. Somehow she felt better just being near the last known place that her two offspring had been. She also felt a drawing. Maybe they would as suddenly reappear as they had disappeared? No matter how unlikely, she was welcomed by the Reeds for as long as she needed the comfort.

Again Sergeant Zer found himself waiting for an answer to his knock upon the front door of the Reeds' cottage. It was also the same time of day as his previous visit. He concluded that it was best not to mention a thing about the trouble in the North. He would play everything down. His job was to ease the tension of this frightened mother.

"Sergeant, what a surprise! More questions of Lenore or just a social call?" Andof was standing tankard in hand. He had taken the day off, deciding to relax and bring a sense of security back to his violated corner of the world.

"Good news, actually. I've come to update Lenore on our findings."

"Well come on in. Good news calls for a tankard. Will you join me? Or are you still on duty?"

"Yes, I will join you, after you...I went off duty awhile ago. Is Lenore in?"

"Yes Mrs. Reed is in the front room sewing with her. Put two females together...all there has been here, is gossip and repairing. They never seem to stop."

Obviously, Andof was far from the perfect husband. Zer noticed even the other night, the smell of drink on him. Humoring him he said:

"Oh my wife is the same. Whenever her sister is 'round I'm just a piece of the furnishings, left out. It's the only time I can smoke my cigar and watch whatever I want."

They both walked down the hallway to the front room. Upon entering Andof announced:

"Lenore, look who is here, and with some good news!"

Lenore's heart missed a beat. Had her youngsters been found?

"Good afternoon again, ladies. Lenore, I have found an impression of a note. Have you ever seen this?" He handed the sheet over. Her eyes devoured the words.

"No. Never!"

"It's my guess then, that whatever has happened, all of them must be alive and well. Probably some burglars broke into the cottage after they had left. Do you have any idea why they would go to Norkleau?"

"I can't understand? Isn't there trouble on the routes to the North? There's no reason to be traveling there. What is my brother up to?"

"It isn't clear. I just wanted you to see the note and

feel a little better as to the whereabouts and safety of your young ones."

The Path to the North

"Thank you Sergeant. It is helpful and my hope is strengthened. I am still a little flabbergasted by all this. Everything is so strange. I'm not sure what to expect next, I pray more good news."

"My sentiments also." He quickly drank more of the

tankard. "I don't mean to be rude, but my wife was expecting me home long ago. I had better be on my way. Just wanted to stop by with the news. I'll continue to keep you updated."

"Thank you, thank you from my heart, Sergeant Zer!"

"No Ma'am. Don't thank me. I'm only doing the job the fine community of Jard pays me to do. I'm soon to be a parent, myself, and I would want to know that others care as much as I do for them. I know your young ones will be fine. It's important at this time that you feel supported and that you know everyone is truly working toward a happy ending. So I will take my leave of you. Don't lose hope, I haven't."

He rose, gave Lenore a hug, shook Mr. and Mrs. Reed's hands and left.

During the brisk walk home, he prayed that all would indeed come to the happy ending he had predicted. There was trouble brewing in the North. Still more dark *evil* was spilling in this direction, towards Jard!

Chapter 9.

Into the dark water Julian was tugged. He held his deepest breath while he spun deeper and along. The panic of being in the water and his disbelief of ever reaching the other side, if there was another side, almost made him cry out. Somehow he maintained enough awareness to know, that wasting his air in a scream could only reduce the chances of surviving. He dug into his faith and belief of Darla.

The rumble of the river was deafening. Somehow the sound was louder under here. Once or twice his eyes opened to see only the bubbles of air, which were also being dragged below the surface with him by this uncompromising master. His shoulders hit a solid object and he was turned over and under. Then a tremendous pressure flushed him into a tunnel. He wrapped his arms over his head and face to protect them from bumping against the solid rock underwater passage. His lungs were starting to strain and his mind screamed for nutritious air! How much longer till he reached the other side? A frenzy set in once more.

"Trust in the Magic." came a voice in his head. "All will soon pass."

Were those his words or someone else's? One more time:

"Trust in the Magic. All will soon pass."

It definitely was the voice of another. It soothed Julian to know that there were greater powers than his own at work here. He was strengthened by its emergence at this moment. He continued to hold his breath, though his lungs wanted to explode and consume new fresh oxygen. In another moment he wondered where

Terence Munsey

Thiunn and Eruinn were, and if they could survive. Numerous thoughts passed before him. He even considered this to be an indication of impending death.

Then there was no more hard surface in the water! He was floating upward surrounded by an open cool subterranean blue. He hadn't noticed when or how, but he was clear of the rocky underpass.

With that thought in mind, Julian began pulling himself through and upward. The current became weaker and weaker. He felt the pressure and wetness change as his arms, then head, went from the heaviness of water to the lightness of the atmospheric world he preferred. He burst out, pleased to have survived the crossing. He continued to kick and pull, trying to keep his mouth above the water, replenishing his soul with deep gaspy strained breaths. He felt like a runner must feel, after finishing a hard race, trying to deal with the sudden stop and recovery. It was fabulous to be alive!

He kept moving himself through the river in the darkness of the cavern till he felt the solid riverbed beneath his feet. He began to move into shallower and shallower water. Finally he found the river's edge and fell exhausted upon its flat dry embankment.

Not long after his own journey, Eruinn and Thiunn, holding each other as firmly as they could, went through the same underwater tunnel. Half way through Eruinn lost grip of his brother. They now were alone. Fear riddled them both. Even as they sank below the surface of the pool, they both knew that they had not, in the suddenness of Darla's push, taken the deepest breath they could. That, coupled with the pressure and bumping of the trip, as well as their severing, made Eruinn waste his air even more in a gargled cry after Thiunn. Not a wise move. Neither expected to survive the crossing.

Again from out of the dark wetness, the foreign voice ensued. This time in the heads of the two young Chosen Ones.

"Trust in the Magic Chosen One. Concentrate on the

goal. Feel the other side. Do not give way to the panic of *evil*. Trust in the Magic. Use its power. Concentrate."

Each of the separated brothers felt that the voice was personally directed at himself. The effort was immense, but each in their own way became calmed and relaxed. They focused upon their goal: to reach the other side alive. The river twisted and pulled them on.

Julian was still lying in the dark upon the bank, when he heard the sound once, then a second time, of the membrane between water and air break. It was like a couple of whales clearing blow holes as they surfaced. Eruinn and Thiunn had made it over!

"Eruinn! Thiunn! Follow my voice. I am here, not far, on shore. I will keep talking to guide you." he kept talking whilst the two responded.

"Uncle...J{between gasping}... thank... good...ness ...I thought...that was... gonna be...it." Eruinn spoke slightly ahead.

"Wow...what a ride...Where are you? Are you okay?" Thiunn was cavalier as always or pretending to be.

"Yes, keep coming in this direction. It's not far. I'm glad you guys are okay. After my experience, I wasn't too hopeful for you."

A hand was stretched out grappling for shore or any object to hold on to. Gradually, four feet found the floor of the riverbed rising up. Julian's voice beacon was above. First Thiunn, then Eruinn were being helped. Soon they were out of the water and being hugged by their loving Uncle! After a few more moments of recovery and the realization that they were safe, Thiunn calmed his Uncle's concern:

"Oh you needn't worry about us. We're fine. Just a little battered and short of breath!" Thiunn was back to his usual good humor.

"Just don't ask me to do that again. If this is the wrong path...well that's too bad. I'm not going back that way!" Eruinn was adamant.

They were all dripping wet and beginning to notice the chill in the cool underground. Julian took a parental tone:

"We will not be able to dry our clothes, so the exertion of walking will keep us from catching a chill. Who has the illuminator?" Julian was happy that they were all safe and sound.

Eruinn suddenly remembered and gave a rapid pat over all his pockets.

"I have it." he called out in the dark.

"Pull it out and give us some light." Thiunn had the tone that brothers give each other to make them feel younger and still a child.

Eruinn exposed the object, which instantly threw a light, displaying the three soaked travelers.

"Other than the drenching, you all look to be in one piece to me. Here, shine the light around. Let's see what we're in for." Julian was curious to know if this passage was similar to the other. It was. A path, like before, followed the river as far as the light permitted view.

"Gentlemen, after you." Thiunn tipped two fingers to his right temple as a sort of playful salute.

"How far do you think it is, Uncle J?" Eruinn was tired.

"Not very. As long as we keep a good pace we will probably arrive by dawn." Julian heard himself speaking, wondering at how he knew what he had just uttered, was correct. But he did know it was correct!

On they went. Three funny wet cats. Every once in awhile, one shaking a limb in an effort to shed some of the water weight. The illuminator was between them and could be seen jostling back and forth, until the darkness of the path enveloped them again. They were almost at their magical destination.

The female had definitely gone. Citol had spent the night searching. There wasn't a trace. How could this be possible? Not one Trooper had seen them leave the Hall or any other part of the Keep. The last known sighting was here, on the Speaker's Balcony. If they had jumped down the twenty lengths, surely they would have been sighted. On top of that, injury was very probable from this height for such small creatures. There must be another explanation. But what? When the Lord Merm sees us arrive empty handed...the concept was too threatening to consider. The sound of approaching steps broke Citol's train of thought. A messenger from the Commander:

"Commander Ruel requests you prepare to join him on the ride to Norkleau, sir."

"Tell the Commander I will be there right away."

Citol was still apprehensive about taking the trip to Norkleau. Ruel had decided it wiser to come in person to report the escape. He even pleaded with the Gott deities to help find the prisoners before the report.

Not long after the message had been delivered, Citol arrived at the main steps of the Keep. He was carrying his travel bag. It was the light efficient case of a field Trooper.

"Reporting and ready, Commander Ruel." the formality had returned between them.

"Mount, and we will ride. There's a hard ride ahead."

He mounted. The party rode through the Keep and over the draw bridge. The bridge guards saluted as their Commander passed.

They rode northwest, taking the fastest route. The day was dark and cloudy. A little nip was in the air. An ominous doom approached.

Darla had walked the tunnels many times. She found little difficulty returning to the secret entrance at the Lake. The Old Ones had improved her sense of hearing and somewhat like a bat, she was more able to navigate her way. She was worried that the Jewel was taken.

Jewel was the name given her weapon. Not just a weapon of metal, also a devise that could focus the magic of its owner. It was linked mentally with her. They could always home to each other, though she was responsible, through her magic of thought, for Jewel's movement.

The symbiosis had taken many years, but now it was complete. Sword and female were of one sense. The sword did not think, it merely shared and acted to improve Darla's 'radar' capabilities. This had proven very useful, especially in low visibility situations, such as now. Jewel kept constant scan for projectiles and pending physical danger to Darla. With it, the chances of injury were tremendously reduced, only because of the advance warning it could give.

Each Chosen One would have a different tool; some used knives, others had used bows. It was not predictable. It always took a long period of time to discover and then finally link beholder with tool. So much depended on the pre-existing individual strengths, weaknesses, and talents of those Chosen.

Darla was nearing the secret entrance. She would press the symbols as Julian and Eruinn had done and carefully address the circumstances she found.

Before long she was at the entrance and opening it. To her amazement, after she peeked around the entrance door, there was a noticeable silence. It was also night. She had expected the night, not the silence.

Creeping out of the passage, she placed a large stone to hold the door open. The door was timed to close once entered or exited and Darla didn't want the bother of trying to open it again, if speediness was necessitated.

Nobody was there on the outside. There was no smell of Gott on the air. Not a fire lit, nor drink perking. What was up? She went near the area that the Troopers had come from before. Looking in all directions she saw and felt no movement.

"Strange? They are no longer encamped here. Maybe it has started! It's essential that I find Jewel and rejoin my friends. They may be in greater danger than first imagined!" Darla was speaking to herself in a low tone.

She quietly went over the area where she and Thiunn had been captured only one night before. She tried to recall the precise location where all were standing, at the time when the alarm to the Troopers had been given. She attempted to remember when she last realized that Jewel was at her side. The best she could recall, was when Julian and Eruinn had found the entrance, opened it and called for the remaining others to come. It was then, that the shot of the cross arrow let go and before she knew it, the door had closed. Eruinn and Julian were gone and Thiunn lay on the ground with the arrow piercing his shoulder. Somewhere the sword had fallen in the skirmish between Trooper and the door closing.

She accepted the reality that a Trooper may have found the sword, but on the other hand, it had been dark and in the rush of the Gotts to continue their purpose, they may have neglected to fully search this area after the capture. She began rifling through the dead leaves and soft loam. She was not successful.

In the moonlit evening she decided to sit and concentrate. She would try to connect with Jewel. She crossed her legs and similar to the event with the Riders, allowed her mind to relax, so she would be able to call upon her magic.

She imagined her Jewel and emphatically called for it. She tried to feel the sword, its size, its shape, its loneliness at being lost. Slowly Darla began to think of the sword lifting and returning her call. She heard a rustling sound which broke the magical trance. Over to one side of the little clearing where the struggle had taken place, she saw a glimmer. Something was drawing her closer. A twinkle caught in the moonlight. She got up and went to see. Not many steps away beneath the soft peat, half covered with leaves, was Jewel.

She leaped forward clutching the weapon as if it were a long lost friend. So happy was she to hold it again. A few moments went by and then Darla reawakened to the urgency of catching up with the others. She had one last look around and seeing nothing of remark, she reentered the secret passage. As she did, she removed the stop she had earlier placed and was instantly hidden behind the solid rock doorway. She would use her best speed to get to Norkleau. Julian would need her help if the Gotts had begun their invasion. She realized that Lord Merm would not have started the movement of his Troops unless he was confident of a trump card up his sleeve. The Key must be in his possession. It would be up to Eruinn, Thiunn and herself to help Julian reclaim it for the Old Ones. She rushed on.

After awhile she came to the fork in the pathway, but unlike Julian, knew which was the right direction to the Lost Palace. Embarking upon it, she touched Jewel.

"It will be up to you to get me to the Palace quickly. The others are in deeper trouble than they are aware. I turn my faith to you. Do not let me down."

Merm was refreshed. The late morning was cloudy bright. His dreams had been so vivid. They were almost real. For some reason he decided to skip breakfast and finish the third warning. Over to the large table he went. Amongst all the books and papers sat the box that held the Key. Leaning over he opened its lid, a short note sounded, like a music box.

"How quaint. In a little, I will understand your magic. Then my Troopers will be unstoppable!"

He had the urge to pick up the Key with his fingers. He was being attracted to it. He resisted. Dorluc's power was still not stronger than his own will. Sitting back down he closed the lid.

"Now to finish that warning." Merm had worked so hard. He now felt very close to its final decipherment. So far he had translated:

Beware the knight dark, he controls . . .

and that had taken a long struggle. For some reason he believed that this warning required more effort to unravel than the others. He would discover the full meaning before lunch. That was his goal. Not one disturbance until that end had been accomplished.

The three traveled at good speed, the rush of the river pulled them psychologically. The winding path had risen, and fallen; now it was running flat. The tiny illuminator was working extremely efficiently, with no sign of fading.

Unlike their beginning at the Lake, there were no ornate caverns or symbols to be seen, just the rock cut tunnel. It was a little before lunch on the outside. The three were tired and hungry.

"Boy, a Sunday meal would go down nicely about now. I'm so hungry I'm losing my appetite!" Thiunn complained.

Julian also noticed the loss of appetite and the reduction of his paunchiness. It was the most exercise ever undertaken by him. If nothing else occurred, he would return a fitter and more handsome Jardian. Maybe Darla would be interested then! It's funny how Cupid's arrow strikes the unaware. From the very first moment of their 'meeting' over five years ago, Julian had had a special attraction to this Lady of the North. It occurred in a flash when their eyes had met. Instantly he wanted her. He had felt her uneasiness. She was so beautiful and he, just a husky Jardian. Perhaps that would change after this adventure?

"Yeah, where are we going to get food down here?"

came Eruinn's irritated reply in the background. The two youngsters were starting to argue.

"We'll steal it from someone at the Lost Palace, Eruinn." Thiunn was sarcastic. He still was immature, even after all that had occurred.

"No need to take that tone, you silly..." Eruinn was cut off.

"Hey! Don't we have enough on our plates without your bickering! You'd think all this would make you better and closer brothers. I realize we're all getting cranky, but remind yourselves where we are. This is not a game. Control the irritation that the hunger causes. We've had too many close calls. Let's not make things any worse!" Julian was right. The two knew that it was the hunger talking.

"Sorry Eruinn, Uncle J. There's no excuse. I just wish we could get our task done and return home. I guess I'm, we're," he was indicating Eruinn and himself, "just homesick and frightened."

"I can sympathize. I'm feeling the same way as well. But if we are to get back, it will be in part dependent upon our cohesion and cooperation. There will be enough challenges to come. We must be a strong uncompromising unit. Strength in considerate toleration!"

Silently they continued. The journey was taking its toll.

Darla was making good way. Unlike the other three, she was used to travel. The lack of food was merely an inconvenience. She would easily suppress her hunger. Drink was no problem. The river was a constant supply of the purest available in all the worlds.

As she continued her advance, the image of Julian appeared amidst her thoughts. There was a power about him. She giggled as she daydreamed of that moment five years before. How much he reminded her of 'the father'.

She saw the moment when their eyes had met. It was

like looking at an old friend, a lover. She felt the surge within, melting slightly in affection. But she was of the Chosen and dare not express her attraction. The yearning years came to her mind. It wasn't fair! She wanted him!

Composing herself, she jumped back to the present. There was no time for this now. The three would need her as fast as she could reconnect with them!

"That's it! At last. But what does it mean? The only warning that I can begin to place is the first. The second was like a child's rhyme, now this?

'Beware the knight dark, he controls when the Lord does not?'

Another riddle! Equally as obtuse as the others. I will ask Rmont his opinion. RMONT! Rmont!" Merm yelled, so that Rmont, who was always close by, would know he could now disturb his Lord.

Rmont knocked and opened the door.

"Here Lord. Can I get you lunch?"

"No you old buzzard, get over here. What do you make of these?"

Rmont hated Merm. The constant abuse. But he had realized great gain by his subservience. His authority and power were only surpassed by Merm himself.

They had joined forces long ago, while still young. Both had been Troopers. Both had ambitions of power. Merm seemed more capable at making things happen, so Rmont had assumed a role in the background. If Merm rose, he would also. The rise hadn't taken long, especially with Rmont maneuvering without Merm's knowledge, in the shadows. This made it harder for Rmont to bear. It was his skill that had prevented disaster at the critical steps. Certainly Merm had a presence and leadership quality, but it was the methodical planning and meetings and promises that had finalized his succession to power. There were still bills to pay. Merm was the front persona, a necessary evil, but Rmont was the brains!

"It is very difficult to apply. They all, except the first one, are very vague." he pointed out the warnings in an attempt to link a message:

**'Beware the Lady <u>and</u> the jewel.
She fully awakens at the first sound of the rock door's Tune.'**

**'Beware the Stoneman's long ago flight.
He with the Key, hides in the fight.'**

**'Beware the knight dark,
he controls when the Lord does not?'**

"We seem to have some connection with this female prisoner that Ruel brings today. We have the Key. That might negate the second."

"And the third might mean you!" Merm's tone was accusing.

"Me! What do you imply Lord?"

"We both know you want power. Perhaps this warns of danger to me from you?" The influence of Dorluc was showing itself.

"But what of the **'knight dark'** reference? Surely you don't suspect me. After all these years and previous opportunities. Really, I like my role and would not care to carry the weight you must bear!"

"Yes." Merm composed himself, "Sorry, you're right, of course Rmont. It's just the frustration of all of these accursed riddles. Why couldn't the writers of these warnings have been more precise?"

Rmont was still rolling the word 'sorry' over in his

mind. Never had Merm apologized. Never! This was not like Merm, even under the circumstances!

"Lord, perhaps a light lunch would help. Commander Ruel will soon arrive. There are preparations to be made."

"Yes. A good idea. The mind can work better when the stomach is full. I will dress. Have my luncheon brought here."

"Yes my Lord. Will there be anything else?"

"Not just yet, but don't wander off. I may have need of you after lunch."

Rmont bowed, turned, and went back up the stairs. As he opened the door he paused, glanced back to Merm who was too self consumed to notice, and gave a menacing stare. He would one day replace this *'Lord'*. He wondered if the third warning had meant his own ascendancy to an absolute rule.

The market square in Jard had been cleared of the booths and stalls of the Festival. The Mayor was to make an announcement at tea time. A large crowd was gathering. Nervously they prattled as to the reason for the sudden halt to the festivities and the announcement which was soon to be made. This was precedent setting for Jard.

Some felt indignant at the ruination of their Festival. They vowed never to support the Mayor in upcoming confirming. They would give their vote to anyone else. Others tried to think of a time when this might have occurred before. Still others waited without saying a word, knowing inside, that great disaster might be at hand.

Soon a party of several Jardians appeared and made their way through the crowd and onto a small raised dais. Area Chief Mal and Sergeant Zer were amongst them. This sent a wave of rumor through the crowd as they passed.

"This must have something to do with the security of

Jard." came one supposition.

"Maybe the danger in the North is worsening!?" came anonymously from the crowd.

The party took its place upon the dais.

"Jardians, neighbors, good friends. Please give me your attention!" The Deputy was trying to prepare the assembly so that the Mayor could speak and be heard.

All the local community press were there jotting down every word, and comment. The newspaper runs had been held on standby, so that the announcement would make the final edition tonight.

"Fellow Jardians...Fellow Jardians. I bring grave news." The noise died down, with shushes of those trying to police the noise makers. The Mayor was starting.

"Louder!" was shouted from the back.

"Fellow Jardians. Today it is my sad duty to have to halt this Summer Festival." booing issued forth.

"This is not done lightly." there was more heckling from the assemblage.

"We are invaded!" there was total silence. Questioning looks were found on each face. "*INVADED!* We have news from the North that the Gott Troops have invaded and captured the bordering villages. Although we are still in the process of confirming and corroborating this information, many may have been killed by this vicious unprovoked attack."

Voices from the now angry and frightened crowd:

"What do you mean unconfirmed?"

"How do you know?"

"What are we to do?"

"Are they coming here?" a few fearful screams were interspersed with the questions.

"Settle down. Panic will not help. I have requested Area Chief Mal here," he turned in the direction of Mal as he announced his name, "to put together a small force of the Guard and travel quickly to the North to investigate and repel any threat. I have also asked the authorities, represented by Sergeant Zer, who once protected our northern lands in the Guard, to help prepare and organize our efforts for defense, if need be, at home here in Jard."

"Please do not panic. I feel certain that this is just a bunch of renegade Gott Troopers and not a full scale invasion. It will be over before it even gets started. I have sent a request to the Gotts by way of intermediaries to confirm or deny the information brought to my attention today by Area Chief Mal and Sergeant Zer."

The Mayor was a good politician. If this turned out to be a false alarm, he would blame these two for the unnecessary halting of the Festival. He would claim that as the Mayor he was obligated, in the best interest of the citizens, to be cautious and follow their advise; that he had to be prepared for the worst, and not be caught off-guard.

"Please return to your homes. Further announcements will be brought to your attention as soon as the need arises." The Mayor motioned for his Deputy to address the crowd. The Deputy stepped forward and spoke:

"For those of you from other villages to the south, it is best to return to your homes quickly, as a precautionary move. Those of you from the northern communities, please remain as our guests until this matter is cleared. Sergeant Zer will speak with you after we have left."

The Mayor raised his hand in order to calm the crowd. He wanted to give his concluding remarks:

"If this is worse than we now suspect, and I don't for a moment believe that it is, remember, we have seen harder times in the past and still we have made it through together. Have courage!"

He turned and left with his party. Zer remained to face the noise and questions. How nice of the Mayor to abandon him, Zer thought!

Merm had just finished his meal, when a knock

came loudly at his chamber door.

"Enter."

"My Lord," It was one of the guards. "Commanders Ruel and Citol have been spotted at the outer walls. They will arrive by early evening."

"Very well. Have Rmont meet them at the main gate and direct them here without delay. Tell the cook to have food prepared and refreshments."

"Yes my Lord."

Chapter 10.

The sorties were too easy. Not one bit of resistance and no sign of the Jard Guard. Where could they all be?

The country-side was full of smoke from the farm-houses having been set ablaze by the advance Troops. The rolling hillside was littered with half turned carts, broken fences and even the occasional dead animal. All this mess would not be cleared away, since it was of no concern to the Gotts. They would rather have the area to be made a little more like their own land. Some of the oldest trees had been lost to the flames. Their charred skeletons lined the hillside. The sky overhead was becoming more darkened. The site was dismal.

The orders for the Division were very clear: secure the routes and test the strength of the enemy. Since travelers had dwindled in the North over the past season, the only inhabitants to be wary of, were the locals. It all had been accomplished in the shortest span of time that any Gott had known! Now they would be digging in. The Gotts were anticipating a response. Patrols were being set up as well, just to keep an eye on the area and the remaining farmers, whose job it now was to service the Gotts. Complete compliance was the only acceptable conduct, or punishment by death resulted.

Citol's division had been hurriedly joined up with the Seventh Division, under Frid, to add to their numbers. It wasn't really needed, but the Gotts were not fully informed of the inability of the South to mobilize. Tosh had been left in command during Citol's absence. Everything had happened so quickly. The orders had arrived from Aug just after the mid point of the night and so the camp mobilized. This was an unexpected good fortune. Tosh would be closely scrutinized by his superiors in this new temporary command. If all went well he was sure to be promoted, maybe even allowed to keep this command and Citol promoted and kept in the Garrison. Tosh knew that Citol would welcome being out of the field. He must be careful to follow orders and have no setbacks. He would send a report to Citol, now that things were less hectic. Tosh relaxed a moment and for the first time noted the smell of burnt straw filling the air. He was pleased to be in Colleg's place. The tavern would make an excellent field headquarters until Commander Citol returned, if he did return. He would send under Citol's seal, his message to Aug:

Sir,
    The advance attack has been a total success. No casualties on our side. We have burnt most of the farms and only kept captive the strong who we need to supply our Troops. We have met no response from the Jard Guard. We make our headquarters at the tavern of Colleg. I await your orders.

signed   *Tosh, Acting Commander.*

All that was left to do now, was dig in, hold the territory, and await orders. It was a pleasant change from just being a Trooper without any real fighting. This was the type of fun Gotts liked best. Being in the service of your world was very boring during peacetime. Here was an opportunity to live! Not one Trooper wished to die, yet by the same token if it was to be, then to die in battle was of great honor. Living on that edge gave the self respect and pride of being a feared Gott Trooper.

Commander Frid had gone out to personally inspect his Troops and assess first hand, the tactical situation. Tosh had, though part of Frid's field entourage, remained behind to settle in and do some paperwork. He also privately decided that he should interrogate Colleg. The innkeeper would have alot of knowledge as to the enemy, their past habits, etc...He sent a Trooper into the kitchen to fetch him.

The Trooper walked through the swing kitchen door and said gruffly:

"You, innkeeper, Commander Tosh demands your presence! Come. Now!"

There was no questioning. The nervous Colleg thought that this was the end. Maybe the bird had been sighted leaving the tavern. It took all his strength to walk past the Trooper and on into the tavern to stand before Tosh.

"Yes sir, may I be of assistance. The food and drink will shortly be ready. I am sorry for the delay, but I only like to serve the best..."

"Please innkeeper, sit down. I have some questions to ask." Tosh indicated the chair opposite him. The room was still dim, even in the daylight. There was the musty smell of drink and there were Troopers at the entrance and nearby. There was no escape. Colleg felt his life go before him.

"What is your name?"

"Colleg, sir. If I have done anything to displease..." again he was cut off.

"Not at all, Colleg. You have owned this tavern long?"

Not sure what to answer, but feeling a little more relieved:

"All my adult life, sir. I..."

"You must hear and know many secrets?"

"Secrets! No never! I just do my..."

"Please relax. I'm not trying to punish here. Only getting to know the innkeeper who will be with us for awhile."

So, the bird wasn't seen! Colleg calmed. But what is this Gott after? How can I use this to my advantage? Colleg hadn't been a survivor this long without the ability to suddenly observe, change, and adapt. He switched from nervous to enterprising, all without a single sign to the untrained eye!

"Sorry sir, I'm just a talker."

"That's fine. That's all I want to do...talk. What can you tell me about the area?"

"I'm not sure what you mean?"

"Well, is it very populated, for example?"

"No. Just the local farmers and the occasional traveler." Colleg would be cautious.

"Much trouble around?"

"Until recently, none at all, but that happens as you know..." he didn't want to offend but at the same time, how do you tell the one causing the trouble that he's the problem!

"I suppose the authorities are able to cope?"

"We hardly have any."

"What? On a border like this, hardly any! I find that hard to believe." Tosh's tone became more threatening.

"You forget sir, that we are a world at peace now. We don't subscribe to violent solutions..." Colleg's sermonette disinterested Tosh.

"Well that peace will certainly help us. Let us hope the rest of the Southlanders are as naive!" Tosh directed this to the overhearing room. The other Troopers who had also overheard Colleg's discourse, found Tosh's comment amusing and a general chuckle filled the room.

"But really Colleg? You expect me to believe that your world would leave unguarded, the border with the Gottlands?"

"We have a signed Treaty…"

"Your Treaty isn't worth the paper it is made of, or ink scribbled upon it. The Treaty was unfair. The Gotts were forced to sign away their heritage, a heritage we are about to re-create! Now, there must be patrols."

Colleg, sensing danger, returned again to his sub-servient attitude.

"Well once in a while."

"How often and where do they report?"

Colleg would have to give this information as accurately as he could. If this Gott believed he was holding back that would determine his end.

"Twice within ten nights, a small contingent stops here. They come directly from Jard and report back there. There are no other authorities in the area. There hasn't been the need. If there is a problem that we cannot deal with, eventually the Jard Guard hears of it and after their patrol, the issue is handled. It has been a good working system. We all respect and value the peace. So much was given in order to secure it, as I am sure you are also aware."

"Yes, but in our case the aftermath was not as fair. We gave up more. We were relegated to the barrenness of the North, stripped of our trading rights, and more. We barely survived. While in the South, there was prosperity!" Realizing he had strayed, Tosh changed back to the current topic. "When was the patrol last here?"

"Abou …"

"Not about. Exactly!"

"One night."

"Thank you Colleg. You are most cooperative. Please return and see to our food."

Colleg rose and started back to the kitchen.

"…Oh by the way." Tosh interjected as Colleg was at

the swing door. "I notice you keep birds." Colleg froze. "I hope you have them only as pets. If you understand my meaning?"

Without acknowledging or turning, he continued into the kitchen. He was alone.

This was the most difficult situation he had ever been in! He wondered if his bird had been able to reach her destination. If so, what would be done. If the patrol that was sent was small, it would be in great danger, or if the note went unnoticed, even more danger. The bird was trained to head to the Area Chief in Jard. It was the tallest structure. Depending upon who found it, the action that resulted could be varied. Jardians tended to be isolationist by nature. They would be reluctant to act swiftly. That was his opinion, at any rate. He would just hope that a scouting mission would be sent secretly. He had done all he could; now it was up to them. It would be everyone for themselves for some time. Colleg resumed his preparations and hoped he could traverse the thin tight rope he now found himself thrown upon.

Tosh had been pleased with the interrogation. The information confirmed many suspicions. The main one dealt with the foolhardiness of the South in its trust in the Treaty and the written peace. So they really had disarmed! No Gott ever truly believed any world would take that section of the treaty seriously. The Gotts hadn't! What fools. This was going to be alot easier than anybody could have anticipated. The Lord would be very happy about this news. When Commander Frid came back, he would apprise him of his conversation with Colleg. They would have use of this innkeeper a little longer.

It would be at least a few more nights before their presence was known to the Jardians. By then, the heavy wheels of the Gott forces would be unstoppable. The Gotts had expected this to be a long campaign, but it was now clear in Tosh's mind, that it was to be a short and easy excursion.

Dorluc was pacing, if you can pace in the Land of No Form. With the unveiling of the last warning, he was anticipating difficulties with the influencing of Merm. Fortunately Merm still hadn't determined the full meaning. It was only a matter of when, not if. Tonight Dorluc would use the most power he could to get the Lord Merm to start using and learning of the magic of the Key. That would unlock the process whereby Dorluc would eventually rule through Merm.

The Key in itself was just a piece of brass, with the knowledge of invincibility being hidden in the *Passwords of Promise*. The Key would unlock their hiding place, thereby giving unlimited access to all the Magic. The Key did, however, possess just enough magic to fool the ignorant beholder. This was a safeguard against unworthy use of the *Passwords*.

The Key gave one the feeling of strength and a few tricks of levitation and disappearance. It was nothing compared to the power of the *Passwords of Promise*.

In order to acquire the power of the Key it had to be worn on gold around the neck. Its aura then spread to that beholder. It was non discriminating. Whosoever wore the Key on gold around their neck, was given the Magic. So much myth and exaggeration existed in the writings of the past, that even more magic was imagined. What fools these mortals can be; so easily taken in by a trinket!

The real quest was to discover and unlock the *Passwords*. They were always hidden near the Key. Dorluc had to influence Merm to look beyond and continue the search for the other. But this was proving difficult to accomplish. Merm was still very single minded.

Another consideration was arising. Dorluc had been noticing more and more a change in the Magic. Magic is an interesting power. If it could be compared to a power source, of any kind. The more items tapping into it, the weaker the current becomes. Lights would not be as bright. Sensing that the Magic had flickered, like the light, ever so slightly, made Dorluc think something else was tapping into it.

At first it had been a tiny drain, but gradually it had grown in steps at least three times. It was normally very intense from the lack of activity since the Old Ones had gone. Even Ho hadn't tapped its source. This time was different. At first Dorluc just thought it was due to his recent use and the intensity required to influence Merm. But after the second change he began to suspect other causes.

One possibility was the Chosen Ones. The opening of the rock door with the tune, according to legend, would awaken any dormant Old Ones within their hosts. These were the Chosen Ones. There were not meant to be any surviving Chosen since the Separation War. It was accepted that they had all perished in that struggle. In fact Dorluc himself had influenced Ho to seek them all out and kill every last member. Dorluc could not seriously consider there to be even one left. They had been too thoroughly routed. Still what was the cause?

Dorluc existed in a world where the concrete was only half present. He could be seen and heard, but not touched. There were others with him. They who were his underlings and followed his every whim. His main 'quarters' was dark and in the center of the room lay a large oblong slab of granite. It was through the stone that he could view wherever and whatever he wished. It was a type of view screen. Magic operated it, fed by the fears and negative energy in the worlds. Whenever he sat using it, his compatriots would kneel around, excitedly seeing the real dimension that they all so terribly missed.

The one common element that bound them together was the hatred they each had of the Old Ones and subsequent good powers, since these were responsible for their banishment. Getting even, whenever the opportunity presented itself, was a treat to be savored.

"So what do you think of our little puppet so far?" Dorluc inquired of his audience.

"He is better than all the ones before. Maybe this one can help set us free again to roam freely."

"I think he will, even though he is a very strong willed mortal. He has the Key and tonight when he sleeps we will again influence his mind to search beyond. I will need your energy to add to the Magic. There seems to be a fluctuation in it lately."

"Yes we have noticed. What does it mean?"

"Something or one, is tapping into it! Where and how hasn't yet been determined." Dorluc would continue to scan the worlds for any indication as to the source. He hadn't considered starting near Norkleau and so was missing the cause under his very nose. As the Magic was revealed to the new young Chosen Ones, the change would be more easily detectable. It again was only a matter of when. So many close situations, as if following a master plan.

"Will this change be of consequence to our goal?"

"There hasn't been a change for as long as I can remember. That is why I have noticed. Perhaps the Magic has been quiet too long and is merely glitching? Who knows? If it grows then we must discover the reason. Our present task with Merm is our priority for the moment."

"We have waited a long time for one such as Merm to surface."

"Don't you think I'm aware of that! I have everything under control! Get out of my sight! You anger me!"

They left the room. Dorluc stood over the viewer.

"So the Magic is changed...whatever the cause. I will eliminate it, just as I will rid myself of these idiots forever!"

He remained, searching the worlds.

In one of the switches of one scene to another, Darla kept appearing, and then in another location: Julian,

Eruinn and Thiunn. The viewer had been set to trace the source of the power change. Dorluc hadn't noticed before, but now he questioned their frequent appearance. He did not know them or their significance; probably another problem, caused by the changes which affected his screen.

They had not always been seen together and even now were not. Three were in some sort of cavern. Dorluc leaned closer. They were of Jard. How quaint to see a Jardian. Silly little mortals he thought.

The screen kept returning to these three no matter how many times it was redirected to restart the search. After several more starts and several more returns, Dorluc began to consider that the screen was on to something.

The three were being careful, as if trying not to be seen or were escaping from something. He put the screen to a wider view.

It was a marvelous cavern lit by a strange familiar glow...The Palace! They were in the Palace! Who were they and what were they doing in the secret Palace? He followed their steps. There were Gott Troopers all over sleeping. Just ahead...! The hiding place of the Key! These three were the cause of the change. Somehow they had the Magic with them and it was growing!

"They're after the Key! The Magic is strong in them. They have the sense of Old Ones, but they are from Jard...Chosen. More of the Chosen!" He burst into a rage so loud, that the others returned to his room to see what had happened.

"*LOOK! THERE IS THE CHANGE! THEY ARE THE CHOSEN OF THE OLD ONES!* They attempt to protect the Key and the *Passwords*!"

"How can you be so sure? They are simple Jardians!"

"How do you explain their presence in the Palace and that the power of their magic is causing the change! They have been Chosen. It would be just like our old friends to play such a trick! What better mortal to lie dormant in, than a Jardian!"

"If what you say is true…"

"Of course it's true. I know how to recognize the threat. It's right there. The screen has also confirmed it by locating these as the cause of the change."

"Then what can we do? If they are Chosen it will be difficult to influence them. The longer we wait the more the Magic grows within them until they are able to protect the Key and all the power of the *Passwords*. We can't do anything."

"Merm, we will have to warn him of their presence before all is lost. We will have to risk exposing ourselves in order to stop this menace. When he takes to his bed tonight, all of us must combine our energy to combat the neutralizing reaction these three have on our influence. There is no time to waste. It must be a strong unified use of our influence. If we can motivate Merm to be on the look out, and also speed him on to discover the *Passwords*. Then we will not have to worry much longer about their threat! They are only three {Dorluc had forgotten the fourth in all the alarm} no match at their present level of magic against our combined front."

"But I thought all the Chosen had been destroyed. How is it that they are still amongst us? Maybe they're just treasure seekers, after the power that their legends tell of, or maybe just adventuring fools…"

"They are of the Old. They are the Chosen. Look at the illuminator the one carries in his hand! Remember them? Where would a simple Jardian obtain such an ancient devise and have enough personal magic to give it the force to cast off the light?! Where?"

There was not a word. The realization of the horror, sinking in each of them.

"Yes…think on it… it is true….Our past is still with us. We will take care from this point, lest they are able to return themselves and combat us till we and our threat are thoroughly disposed of. There is greater magic than even we, are cognizant."

The tunnel wound on and on. All three were beginning to wonder whether this was the correct pathway. The river still followed or lead, depending upon your view. The darkness was complete, save for the tiny ball of light surrounding them. It was just past dawn on the outside.

Gradually, as before, the path began to separate from the river and move to a sharper and sharper incline. Soon the three were on all fours climbing upward, again a plateau. This time there were no steps. The little light revealed just a wide empty space. They all strained to see as far as possible.

"Over there. Another peep hole. See the narrow light." Julian was first to spot the beam of outside light.

"Thank the stars we are there."

"Mind Eruinn, that's what we thought last time. Let's get closer and take a peek to the other side." Julian rushed towards the light.

All were eager to see through. Julian was first. On the other side was a dimly lit cavern. There were two stone pillars to each side blocking a complete view, but down the middle, a pathway was visible. There were Troopers all over! Eruinn then Thiunn had their chance, then all three sat with their backs to the secret door. They were dismayed.

"Nothing can be easy. Why are all these Troopers here? Are we back in Aug? Or is this the Lost Palace?" Eruinn spoke out loud.

"If it's the Palace and Troopers are here, then we may be too late. Merm might already have the Key."

"Yes that's a possibility Uncle J., but it's also good," Thiunn was letting his stomach think, "because there will be food nearby that we can steal!"

With the mention of food, the others became acutely aware of their own hunger.

"We should try to get something to eat soon or we will have no energy to finish our task." Julian agreed with Thiunn's sentiments.

"How do we go about it? It will be tricky."

"We open the door, and have a scout around, get what we can and return here. From there on we can plan depending upon the findings."

"Uncle Julian, will this door operate the same as the other?"

"Eruinn, place the light in front of this door and look for the symbols."

Eruinn complied, and within moments of applying the light, the symbols were clearly seen in the same location as the other door.

"There they are." Julian drew the youngster's attention. "This time, one of us will remain by the door to make certain it stays open till the other two get back."

As it was to be Julian's responsibility to care for the Key, it was agreed that the two apprentices would venture amongst the Troopers.

The plan was to carefully creep out and find something to eat, then return. They all took a deep breath and pushed the symbols, not really knowing what to expect. The door opened quietly and out they stepped.

They were in some type of enclosed area hidden from the view of the Troopers. It was a base chamber to the two columns. Two giant men were in a seated position, pedestaled by the columns. They were holding something in their hands. There was a roof above and on the far wall under this alcove, straight ahead, a very tiny flat framed door, like a safe that was centrally positioned.

The secret passage door opened into a shadowy corner. As the two turned to their right, they could see through the covered place a marvelous cavern, which had a strange light emitting from its walls. About forty lengths farther ahead was a set of stairs leading to a tunnel pathway, or so they assumed.

The Troopers were not watching, but just talking

with each other and generally wasting time. They obviously weren't awaiting guests. There was a table fifteen lengths to the right. Upon it, steaming canisters and below, a few containers, of what the two felt was food. They could crawl along the cavern wall in the shadows, take a canister and return with it to their lair. They wouldn't be noticed if they went without making a sound.

Eruinn got onto his hands and knees first and started to the table. Thiunn followed. They kept well into the dark gap that the cavern light missed, between the wall and the floor. They moved silently, constantly checking in case a Trooper spotted them. There was no one near. Thank the stars they were so small in comparison to the Gotts. They would pass as a small animal unnoticed, like the many scavengers that lived around the Gott encampments. How did they know this? Both were getting much new knowledge since their underwater crossing. They reached the gigantic table. Eruinn took the two smallest containers, passed one to his brother and they turned back. Still no notice. Keeping within the dark shadow, they came back to the pillars and the passage entrance. Julian was waiting. He ushered them in and slowly shut the door. The first task was done. It had been too easy to believe. They would sit and have their first meal in a long while!

"I can't understand how we did that so easily." Thiunn was placing his container on the floor.

"Don't question good fortune. Let's see what it is we're about to eat." Eruinn had also put down his canister and Julian was about to open them up.

Julian pried the lids off. It was a stew of sorts. It would do. They were hungry.

"But what are we to eat with? We don't have any spoons."

"I am impressed with your manners Thiunn. We will make do with these." Julian held up eight dirty fingers, "These will be the only utensils required. We aren't exactly at a formal setting here. The most important thing is to get food into us and right away. After we eat, we will rest awhile. Maybe by then Darla will have caught up with us and be able to offer some advise as to our next move.

While you two were gone, I snuck over to the tiny framed door on the far wall. It has recently been opened. Inside was nothing but a keyhole almost filled with dust and the dusty outline of a square object. I think Merm has the Key!"

"Oh no! It could be anywhere. How are we going to know where to find it?"

"Eruinn, there will be a way, right Uncle J?"

"I hope so. Remember Darla said it would be better if the Key was still untouched. Who knows what magic Merm has acquired by now? Maybe he isn't even here?"

"He's here. This is where Darla and I were to be brought today, to the castle at Norkleau. So the Key and Merm will be here, and somewhere in this castle. All we will have to do is walk by all these Troopers, past all the other Gotts we see in the street, find the castle, walk into it, find Merm and the Key."

"We get the picture." cut in Eruinn, "Nobody said it would be easy. Maybe as Uncle Julian says, Darla will be here soon and be able to show us a way?"

"Are we gonna eat or discuss the time away? Dig in!"

Julian started. It was warm, lumpy and gooey. He held his hand in front of his face, smelled the substance and then tasted with trepidation a small lump. The other two stood waiting upon the reaction.

"Uhmmm...not bad. Tastes a bit salty, but close to a Jardian stew. Once you get passed the texture and looks, it's very palatable. Here Eruinn, you try."

Eruinn dug his hand into the lumpy slime, drew it to his face, closed his eyes and popped it into his mouth.

"You're right. It isn't bad! Come on Thiunn, have some before it's all gone!"

Thiunn took a heaping handful and ate without hesitation. He was nodding his head in agreement as his brother and Uncle hungrily slurped in more.

They ate till they were so full that one more handful would burst their now bulging stomachs! They would take some time to rest and prepare for the next phase of their journey.

"Eruinn leave the illuminator in front of us on the ground. If Darla arrives she will be able to know where we are. Put the lid back on the container. Darla will be grateful for the food. I suggest we all get a short rest." Julian lay back closed his eyes and drifted off into a pleasant sleep.

Thiunn rolled onto his side and within no time Eruinn and he had joined their Uncle, all three were fast asleep.

- - - - - - - - - - - - - - - - - -

Darla made record time on the passage to Norkleau. She never stopped to rest. It was supper time on the outside by the time she came to the steep incline. Which way did they go?

There was a plateau ahead which Darla knew led to the Lost Palace and there was to the left, just out of the main view, another passage. The second passage had been tunneled out by the descendants of the Old Ones. It linked the castle at Norkleau to this subterranean world.

After some thought, Darla concluded that the others would have gone straight for the beam of light and missed the second passage. As she paused, she saw the faint glow of the illuminator. What a relief. There they were. It would have been impossible to find them if they had taken the second passage. It lead directly into the main chamber of the castle, where capture was the most likely outcome, since its door was under the stairwell and in clear view. There was no peep hole to enable the tunnel traveler to see where they were enter-ing and who would be in the chamber to greet them. Its original function was one of an escape route not an entrance point.

Darla proceeded forward. Julian, Eruinn, Thiunn were on the floor asleep. Not waking any of them, Darla noticed the smell of food and the container near the illuminator. She picked up the container and removed the lid:

"Ah...Gott stew it looks like. Anyway, it tastes good. I must have been expected."

She sat down and noisily began to wolf down the repast. She became revitalized. It was the first thing she had to eat since Thiunn's and her incarceration in Lord's Keep. The noise awoke Julian, who cautiously opened one eye then the other. It might be a...who knows who it might..."D!...I mean... Darla!" he corrected his half awake weary mind. "How long have you been here? Did you find your sword? Are you okay?"

"Relax Julian. It is all okay." she placed her hand upon the sword as she spoke. "We're fine, but where did you get the Gott Stew?"

"Eruinn and Thiunn went into the cavern and... borrowed some, {in good spirits} while I manned the passage doorway. We didn't want to be locked out!"

"You are all becoming excellent adventurers. Why I don't believe you really need me...{there was a double meaning}."

"Need you! We can't go forward without you! There's a complication."

"Like what?"

"The Key is gone."

"How do you know?"

"While the youngsters were out scavenging, I had a look in the hiding place of the Key. It's directly opposite the opening here." He indicated beyond the now closed door. "Someone has removed the contents of the wall safe."

"But you've never seen it before."

"I know, but there was one little square area in the center without dust. It was clean, whereas the rest of the inside was dusty and undisturbed. Now, there are all these Troopers in this cavern. Two plus two..."

"Do you think Merm has it!?"

"Yes."

"This is a little more complicated and dangerous. We have to get the Key before it can be fully used. The Troops to the south are on the move. They may already have started their invasion, now that Merm feels the confidence of the Key. But what of the *Passwords of Promise*?"

"What *Passwords*?"

"The real magic of the Key. Little books with the *Passwords* written down. They would be near the Key."

"The only other thing in the safe was a dust filled hole or crack. I thought it was just the settling of the structure causing a fissure."

"We will have to look. Care to join me?"

Seeing no alternative Julian nodded in agreement adding, "What about...?" He pointed out Eruinn and Thiunn who still lay asleep."

"They will be safe. We will only be gone moments."

"After you." Julian was teasing. They both approached the passage door and peered through. Seeing it clear, they pressed the symbols to open it. All was the same as before.

They crept the short distance to what was the wall safe, opened the tiny framed safe door and examined the inside. It was as Julian described.

The dust was everywhere uninterrupted except for the square area. On the back was the 'fissure'. Darla was careful not to change a thing.

"I think we should get out of here. Someone is coming," Julian informed.

Half dazed with the ramifications of the findings, Darla turned, "the *Passwords* are safe for now, but we need that Key to remove them. That is when your job, as all the others before you, begins. Let's get out of here!"

Retracing their steps they passed through the secret passage door, back to where the two youngsters slept.

"We will wake them, but first, the 'fissure' is an inner safe. The dust has filled the keyhole. Merm mustn't have seen it. We have some time on our side. The Key is nothing compared to the Magic of the *Passwords*. We will have to enter the castle room and discover the whereabouts of the Key."

Darla was realizing her greatest fears. Something about this next phase of the journey was to her, prescient. Evil eyes were upon them all!

Chapter 11.

Commanders Ruel and Citol upon their arrival were escorted to the Lord Merm's castle chamber. Both were extremely agitated. An armed guard had greeted them along with Rmont, to take charge of the prisoners. Rmont hadn't said a word since meeting them prisonerless.

"Enter!" Merm was seated at his table.

The party descended into the room to the greetings of a proud father.

"Commanders, please approach. This is excellent work you have performed." the room door having closed behind them, Merm glowered.

"Why haven't you allowed the prisoners to enter? Trooper, bring them in!"

The Trooper wasn't sure what to do and looked to Rmont for help.

"My Lord. It seems they have escaped." after Rmont uttered that sentence, the Commanders cowered in anticipation of a cruel abasement.

"Is this true, Commander Ruel?"

"Yes my Lord...during the night...from the dungeons. I don't know how..."

"From the dungeons of the Keep? That is unheard of! How is this possible?"

"There was outside help, my Lord. They must have used a secret entrance. They came and went leaving no trace. There was nothing we could do. One of the cell guards thought he heard mention of Norkleau as their destination."

"Norkleau? Why here? That's absurd. He was probably drunk!"

"Yes my Lord."

"What is your part in all of this?" he asked Citol.

"I captured and brought them to Lord's Keep to be delivered here, my Lord." Citol would extricate himself by burying Ruel. "I thought all would be safe in Commander Ruel's hands. No one has ever escaped the Keep dungeons."

The Lord was showing great restraint. He had heard the rumors of many secret passages within the Keep and even the castle here at Norkleau, but there had never been any occurrence of their use since the Gott controlled these lands. As upset as he was, he didn't want to alienate or intimidate his Commanders by being what might appear unfair and cruel to Ruel, who had done his best under the circumstances. If he had not come in person to deliver the bad tidings, then that would have been a different story.

"Commander Ruel."

"Yes, my Lord Merm." He clicked his heals and stood to attention to accept his fate with the honor of his position.

"Although I am not pleased with this unfortunate mishap, I realize that it was neither your, nor Commander Citol's fault. There is more to this than meets the eye. Powerful Magic is at hand. If what your cell guard says is true, then we will all have another opportunity to deal with them. You both must be hungry and tired. Rmont will show you to your quarters. Join me for supper after you've settled. Dismissed."

"Thank you my Lord."

"Thank you, Lord."

Both left. Rmont remained behind. "I'll be right with you Commanders. Please wait outside."

"Well, what is it?"

"Lord, do you think the female would come here? What strong purpose would she have?"

"I don't believe this female or her handful of accomplices will venture within these walls. By now they are all back in their homes in the South. Sooner or later we will come across them as we invade farther. If they are coming here, I don't see the danger yet. In either event, double the guard as a precaution. They won't slip through our veteran hands."

"Was it a good example not to punish Ruel? Think of the precedent it sets."

"I have my reasons and I won't explain them here to you. I need friends at this point, not enemies! Punishing them now would have done more harm to our cause and my leadership. They did their duty as best they could under the circumstances. You forget that we are not dealing with the ordinary and can't therefore react in the same manner."

"Do you believe then that the female is part of all this and the Key?"

"All I know is, I will be prudent in my choices over the next while. When I know for a certainty the facts, then I will act accordingly. You had better see our guests to their quarters. Join me with them as soon as possible in the East Hall. It will be an early eve. In the morning we will see what magic this Key can give."

"Yes, my Lord. Will everything be all right?" Indicating the box and Key.

"Don't be so worried, nothing will happen here. We are not Commanders Ruel or Citol. Now hurry, I don't wish to wait all night. I'll see you shortly. Do not discuss with them anything of this matter of magic or Keys. The longer it remains secret, the better. There is much to understand of its power."

"Yes Lord." Rmont went up the stairs and out the door.

"So… We have some competition. I'll have to raise the stakes a bit." Merm didn't trust anyone, especially after the warnings. He would take some precautions of his own, just as a safe guard.

Dinner was the usual fare. All were seated around a rectangular solid rosewood table on heavy high back chairs that were carved with spirals to match the castle's. Servers waited behind a few lengths, off by the walls of the Hall. There were three chandeliers and tapestries hanging from ceiling to floor. The floor was as every floor, sandstone. Windows lined the uppermost portion near the 'V' roof, with its heavy beams.

The conversation was slow and mainly hovered on the reports of the Troops moving in the South.

"The exercise has met with no opposition to speak of and Frid reports all goals accomplished. He is very surprised." Rmont was trying to keep the table from falling to silence. Merm hadn't said a word.

"Commander Citol, what is your evaluation? Being a Field Commander, your views would be of value."

"Thank you. I have always believed the South had disarmed completely. It's as if their lack of attention to any issue dealing with war, in their minds, will make the inevitability of its reoccurrence an unlikelihood. I believe the reports. They have been caught unaware."

"And our next step?" Rmont persisted.

"Reinforce and group a large contingent at our present positions and then spearhead in with one massive swoop to all the Southlands. If we don't give them a chance to arm, casualties will be minimal on our side. We would spend a week, maybe two in the whole operation."

"And if we wait?" Merm cut in before Rmont continued.

"Casualties will dramatically increase. Once the Jard Guard has been called up, it will take months longer to win. But either way we will win, under your leadership, my Lord."

"I agree with Citol's evaluation. We must move while surprise is still with us. The Guard is a formidable fighting force when completely mobilized." Ruel added.

"But if they are disbanded, surely they're organization under these circumstances would be chaotic, benefiting our advance?" Merm wasn't going to mention the security of the win as long as he had the magic of the Key on his side. There was no need to rush.

"They never completely disband, but go into an active reserve. It would not take more than a day to reorganize them. Certainly new weapons and supplies would take longer, but each reservist would have enough to carry him through the first onslaught. When Citol says that they disarmed, it doesn't mean that they destroyed all existing weaponry, they just stopped creating newer, or replenishing the older stockpiles. That was the gist of the Treaty. They obviously have lived to its terms. Do not mistake the present lack of response to imply a total disarmament. That is not the case. Dormancy would be a better interpretation of the lack of response, not lack of ability. If they are given even the shortest time, they will be a force to contend with, even with our present advantage." Ruel was well versed in the ways of the Southern Jardian Guard.

Merm remained in thought and they all continued to converse as they supped.

"What about this female and friends, my Lord? What part does she play in all this?" the question came from Citol. He was still digging at Ruel. A tension was building.

Breaking his silence this question created, Merm decided he would be creative:

"It was drawn to my attention that she was a courier, for the authorities in Jard, including the Guard. Apparently she is carrying information on our Troop movements. I would like this information to not get to Jard."

"But she carried no letters. We found her bag. It was filled with roots and herbs. She is a shaman of sorts."

Merm found this an interesting addendum.

"A shaman? Why?"

"Jard has a Summer Festival at this time of year and all the naturopaths collect to compare potions and sell remedies. She must have been headed in that direction. My scouts have reported that she went to a local stonemason's there. Next, she is captured near the Lake. A very odd..." Citol continued but Merm's and Rmont's mind went to the warnings! Perhaps then she is spying on us? All the more reason to apprehend her and her party. Merm was worried, not for the spying, but for the discovery of the second warning.

"Who is this stonemason? Why would she visit him?"

"We don't know, my Lord. All we can surmise from the report is that he is a simple Jardian of little significance. It's probably just a safe harbor during the storm. We have no other intelligence. Why he disappeared is unknown. He could have been alerted to our scouts and simply gone into flight?"

"Flight?"

"Yes Lord. In order not to be found. He must have been told by the female that he could be in danger. Who knows? Maybe he just went on a vacation."

"Maybe. Still, if she resurfaces I want her stopped." Merm was connecting the warnings and all these coincidences with names and words. He would re-examine the warnings right after the meal, before he slept. The conversation went to other topics. Finally all was finished.

"Gentlemen. If you'll excuse me. I still have some work to do before I retire. Feel free to remain. I will see you at breakfast. Goodnight." As Merm rose, they all stood and bid him a pleasant eve. Merm left the hall, and within moments was back in his chamber.

'Beware the Lady <u>and</u> the jewel.
She fully awakens at the first sound of the
rock door's Tune.'

'Beware the Stoneman's long ago flight. He
with the Key, hides in the fight.'

Merm sat at the table overlooking the warnings. He left orders that no one disturb him for any reason. The meaning of the two warnings was getting more clear. Definitely others were after 'his' Key. Somehow the female and this Jardian were involved and probably on their way to find the Key. But they wouldn't find it. He had already removed it from the box and placed it around his neck, as a precaution against thieves.

Ever since placing the Key on the gold chain he always wore, he had begun to feel different. He needed an early night. In the morning he would feel better.

These warnings were a frustration. After a long contemplation, coupled with the funny way he was beginning to feel, Merm decided to call it a night. He changed and got into his bed. All would be clearer in the morning.

As he drifted off, his thoughts lingered on his fears. He had worked so hard to get here and to obtain the Key. He didn't want to loose it all just as he was so close. He needed some insurance, and the Magic of the Key would provide it. Tomorrow he would discover its secrets. He would turn to the Forbidden Books for help in unlocking the great Magic. This thought reassured him. It also reassured the awaiting Dorluc.

The small contingent of the Jard Guard was waiting in the briefing room. They had heard all the rumor of war and invasion. The Area Chief was on his way to speak directly with them and brief them on this mission.

This small force was an elite group who in the past had been used to efficiently settle any problems in the North rapidly and with little disturbance. They were skilled professionals, career Guardsmen, kept on even after the Separation War Treaty had been signed, to act as a civilian peace keeping tactical unit. Mal would use them well on this eve of impending *evil*.

"Good evening. Please remain seated." Mal came

into the room and proceeded to the podium. His aide placed a map of the area of concern on the wall board.

"I'll get right to it. There is a report of invasion in the North. A large Gott force has captured the territory." He showed on the map. "From here to here. We don't know much. That's your job. You are to proceed to the area and return with confirmation of the invasion and all other pertinent details. You have one night to report."

There was a grumbling.

"I know it's alot, but if we are under attack, we need to react with speed. Equally, if it is a false alarm, we can then stop the regrouping of the force without having caused too much upset. Let me stress the importance of a speedy completion of your mission. Any questions?"

"Sir, if this invasion is confirmed are we to engage the enemy?"

"No. Absolutely not! If it is confirmed, under no circumstances reveal yourselves. That is an order!"

"What if we're sighted?"

"That's why I'm sending this veteran group. DO NOT get sighted! If it is an invasion, the longer the Gotts think us unprepared, the better the chances of defending ourselves and eventually repelling their attack."

There wasn't another question.

"You have your orders. Best of luck go with you."

Mal exited the room. They would leave immediately.

- - - - - - - - - - - - - - - - - -

It was a clear cold night. The moon was full and the stars bright. The unit of ten had been setting double time on their trek North. They were almost at Colleg's tavern. So far there was nothing out of the ordinary. Just the sleepy rolling farmlands, bordered by rows of magnificent trees. They slowed their pace in order to prevent as much noise as they could. They were traveling light and without supplies. The closer they got to the tavern, the more they noticed a smell of a fire burning.

"It must be Colleg up late preparing pies for the next day." one turned to another and whispered.

"I'm gonna have a piece of 'that' when we arrive." He was referring to the smell of something cooking. "This traveling around the country-side is just a red herring."

"Quiet! Not a sound till I clear it!" The Unit Captain was not pleased with their talking. He was worried about what might be out in the area.

They rounded the last curve and were in view of Colleg's through the trees. There were many horses, a few tents, and—Gotts!

The Captain signaled an urgent stop and dispersed his ten into the shelter of the surrounding forest. He huddled with his second.

"What do you think? Could just be a small Gott Troop stopping for the night?"

"This far south Captain? I don't like it at all."

"Then we'll have to get as close as we can. You take two around there." He pointed out the far side where the encampment lay. "I'll send a few farther up into the farmland and go with two as close to the tavern as is safe. We'll meet back here. Don't get caught and hurry back. Just have a look see."

"Okay." He chose two and went off.

The Captain found the rest of his unit, gave them their instructions, and all set off in their sections to gather more information. They were all told to be careful and quiet. Not one wanted to be the first Guard responsible for upsetting the plan and causing their presence to be known by the Gotts! It would be the most dishonorable and unforgivable act for a member of this elite group!

The Second and his two made their way tree by tree, until they came within earshot of the tents. It was the

Gotts all right. They were heavily armed, but it was impossible to determine their purpose.

The encampment was larger than it appeared from the other side. This was not a small force! They noticed sentries on their way in this direction. It would be wise to return to the others.

The few others that went ahead, also proceeded with care and camouflaged their movements. As they went farther north, the smell of burning and, as only a fighter would know, the smell of death, was strong. It was difficult to make out, but many leveled cottages were still glowing embers of their former selves. An odd cart lay deserted. An eeriness loomed. All was not right. The farther they went, the more they noticed trampled crops and ruts in the fields. A great number had passed through very recently. They had seen enough.

The Captain and his two managed to work their way to the side window of the tavern. There was light within and they would have to show vigilance in their motion. Removing his hat while two kept watch, the Captain glimpsed through the bottom pane into the main dwelling. There were Gott Troopers standing guard and at a table overlooking some large papers that the Captain took for map. There was another Gott off to one side, deep in thought. The reports were confirmed. He motioned his scouts to return and regroup with the other two sections. One by one they crept back to the trees.

Finally the Unit was regrouped. Each quickly reported what they had viewed.

"We have stumbled onto their headquarters. It's pointless to remain. Let's be careful upon our return. So far no one is alerted."

They used the shadows to retreat. The impact of their discoveries added a greater urgency to their trip.

By dawn, the Unit headed by the Captain, were seated in the briefing room, drinking a hot beverage and eating small cakes, awaiting again the arrival of Mal.

"Good Morning." the Area Chief greeted as he entered with his aide. "I have to commend you all on the expeditious completion of this mission. Please Captain, give me your report."

The meeting was more informal this time. All remained seated. "Sir... We confirm the invasion. The Gotts have encamped with great numbers, here, here and here." He had walked to the wall map and was pointing them out. "There is destruction and farmlands have been crossed with horse and wheel. It was hard to determine numbers in the dark. The tavern has become a headquarters. By all indications they are digging in, preparing for a long stay."

"Any current threat?"

"Hard to say, sir. I would recommend a total recalling of the Guard, if there is time."

"We've already done the preliminary call. I will advise the authorities to instate a complete communication. How long do we have?"

"A night or so, maybe less. They are digging in, which leads me to believe they are uncertain as to our capabilities. The Gotts could have overrun us in one movement if they hadn't stopped. Their intelligence is obviously lacking, or there is another hold up unknown to us at this time."

"This is grave news. Why this sudden mobilization?"

"Unknown Sir."

"Captain, you and your Unit have served beyond the call. Your information and speed may be the determining factor in our survival. Good work. I must report to the Mayor." He rose, saluted the Unit, and hurriedly made his way to the Mayor. It had been a hard night for everyone!

The Mayor had slept very little over the past night, anxiously awaiting Area Chief Mal's dispatch. He hadn't expected him to bring it in person. He knew at first sight of him entering the office, that the invasion was confirmed. Jard's peaceful life was in jeopardy! Could he survive this and get back into office?

"Mal, you're up early. The news?"

"Confirmed, Mr. Mayor."

"How extensive?"

Mal closed the office door.

"Sir, we will be lucky if we can talk together like this in another two nights. Everything will depend on our abilities to mobilize and set up a defense."

He conveyed the complete report he had received from his scout unit. The Mayor sat, under the weight of the detail.

"The First Division will be ready to march North today, but the Second through Fourth will each need longer. We are greatly disadvantaged in supply. Even if we defend, it will require powers beyond our present capabilities to push the Gotts back. I fear our efforts will act only as a short delay."

"We will have surprise on our side. They do not expect a threat from us. Maybe that will be enough?"

"Maybe." Both the Mayor and the Area Chief knew better.

"It is best we don't speak of this to others. It would be better to keep morale high. Knowing the futility of our defense will not ameliorate matters."

"Quite so. If we must go down let it be with our spirits high!"

"Mr. Mayor, I will lead the First Division. They will need my experience to make any worth while stand."

"And what are we to do here without you?"

"Sergeant Zer has had ample experience. He will best be used organizing here. We will work well together over the distance. I trust him."

"May the Magic of the Old Ones protect you."

Mal hadn't heard that old expression in years. He thanked the Mayor and proceeded to prepare his Division for departure.

Not long after the meeting with the Mayor and without any fanfare the First Jardian Division marched out of their barracks on the way to protect their world. It was surprising how uniform they appeared, as if they had been drilling everyday. They were marching and singing the old Jard Guard song. How many would return, or whether they could be successful was uncertain. Soon they were out of sight and Jard would turn to its own arrangements for security against the Gotts. A serious tone had replaced the frivolity of the Summer Festival.

How quickly all the harmony had changed. Jardians old and young alike were not sure which way to turn. Was this to be the end or a newer beginning?

Lenore was tearful again.

"My youngsters! What will happen to them? Will they survive and where will they know to find me, if the worst happens? Will I ever see them?"

"Now, now. Everything will work out fine in the end. You must come with us away from Jard. It will not be safe to remain. My brother has a cottage far to the south. It will be safer to house ourselves there. I am convinced that your youngsters will seek you out. We will leave word with the authorities and a note in your cottage."

"But what if they are lost and need me here?"

"All will be fine. If you remain here and the Gotts invade deeper, what will be left for your youngsters to find? Nothing? You must come, for their sake, if not your own."

"She is right." Mr. Reed added. "The Gotts do not take prisoners. Your two will be fine, but I'm afraid you wouldn't have much hope here under the Gotts. We must all go south. We will keep our ears open for news of them. This will be no place for women and children."

"Please Lenore! Have faith in the future! We must go now!"

Chapter 12.

The plan was to arrive in the early hours before dawn and attack the unaware Troops while their numbers were still relatively small. If the Jard Guard could manage this, it would send a shock wave all the way to Lord Merm. He would be forced to reevaluate his tactics, being now on the defensive. It was brilliant. Mal knew his stuff. They were to set up just south of Colleg's, out of view of the Gotts advance watch. The watch hadn't really been put into effect yet, but Mal wasn't aware of this failure on the part of the Gotts.

Upon reaching their destination, Mal called together his Unit Commanders to explain the action they each would take.

"Surprise is our weapon. The Gotts have assumed our inability to respond. They have also discounted any significant 'Guard' as a factor. We must appear larger than we are, attacking in many groups from many directions. If we can fool them into thinking we are a formidable foe, we might be able to pull this one off. Of course, they will reinforce after, but we will worry about that later. This might give us enough time to get more Guard help. Remember they are feeling invincible and are making mistakes based upon their recent triumph. Each of us must equal six of them! The attack must be completed before sunrise. That gives us lots of time. If we can rout them with our surprise, then we will have done well! Our other goal is to capture their headquarters. That will give us more leverage and add, hopefully, to their confusion. I don't know how long we will be able to hold the regained territory, or if we can. I also don't know how long till a counter attack will take place, but our initial attack will sure bloody their noses and make them think twice! Questions?" Mal had spoken with a sense of urgency.

"Are we to take prisoners?"

"Other than at the tavern, no. I'm afraid we can't afford that luxury. If we are to protect the South, we will have to be barbaric, at least for now."

"What if we're expected?"

There was no response. All then realized the profundity of what might well be their last battle. If they weren't successful, there just wasn't an alternative.

"We will use the tavern as our base, if we are successful. Let's show them the 'Guard' of legend. Make them fearful of our imagined Magic of Old. The odds appear difficult, but that won't deter us from what we know we are capable of!" Mal then gave the specific objectives to each of his Unit Commanders. His personal assignment would be the taking of the tavern.

"Wake up you two sleepy lugs! This isn't a vacation!" Darla was fooling with them. It was time to set upon the other path.

They opened their light starved eyes.

"Darla! Whe...When did you get here?" Thiunn rose and Eruinn sat upright.

"Your Uncle and I have been poking around outside for awhile. Now it's your turn."

"How was the outside?" Eruinn mumbled. He was meaning the worlds outside the underground passage. Darla understood his confusion.

"It's after supper time, the darkness of the night has fallen, if that's what you really wanted to know. You look a little disoriented. The Gotts have begun their invasion. The Key is in the possession of Lord Merm. Our time is almost gone."

"Oh...Is that all? Eruinn was groggily awakening.

"What do we do now, Darla?" Thiunn was eager to move. Anything to get back outside to his sunlit world!

"We will enter the castle and find the Key. Then it is up to your Uncle to secure the *Passwords* as well."

"And where are they?"

"The less you know about them the better. If you are caught you will not be of any assistance to the *evil*. But don't get caught, if you can help it!"

A chill ran up the youngsters' spines.

"We don't plan on it." they both responded closely together.

"How are you two young apprentices feeling? Noticed any changes?" Darla was curious as to what level of the Magic they had so far reached and could in the future absorb. They were passed the test and on the way of the Chosen.

"A little different. I can sense more and there's tingling inside."

"Me too." Eruinn interjected. "But I also have a sense of power or strength. Not physical, more spiritual or mental. I feel like I might be able to do something extraordinary, but I don't know what?"

"Yeah. Like, I can reach out and make things happen, without actually being there?" Thiunn was looking inward as he tried to explain the newness of all that he was going through. It was hard to explain. There had not been enough time of exposure to the changes for him to express the experience.

"Good. It will be a little longer before you are understanding. There will come a point where it will happen and you will be in control, without any conscious effort. Are you ready to continue?"

Both nodded in consent.

"This is our plan."

All of them gathered near and listened as Darla spoke. She told of the need to enter the castle, find Merm's chamber, and then the Key. She knew that the Key would be with Merm and that he would be using the inner chamber of the Norkleau Castle. She wasn't sure how she knew of all this, it was just some inner knowledge. It was all part of the inner dormant experiences of all those before and still within her mind.

Norkleau had been the original seat of the Magic and power of the Old Ones. Great knowledge was continued and kept within the Chosen of this ancient center. Darla, like many before had inherited through her being Chosen, all of the knowledge of the castle and its layout. The inner sense would release the required amount of knowing at the time when needed and would lead her and the youngsters to Merm and the Key. Now was the time!

"Eruinn, Thiunn and I will go on to the castle and hopefully get the Key. Julian will stay here and wait and I *mean* wait. Do nothing else! We will take the illuminator. It is our only source of light. You will have to remain, with only the glow through the peep hole to light your spirit. You *must* be here upon our return. Only you can unlock the *Passwords* safely. It is your calling. We are merely the go-betweens. If something goes wrong, one of us will come back.

Only two of us will enter the castle chamber of Merm. The other will wait behind the secret passage door."

"How will we know where to look? How do we know the Key will be there?"

"We don't Eruinn, but if you were the Lord Merm, and you found the Key, where would you most likely keep it?"

"With me at all times. I wouldn't trust a soul."

"Exactly. So Merm's room is the best place to start. If it's not there…we will just have to pray that it is!"

"But how do we know where this chamber is and that Merm is using it?" Eruinn did not understand Darla's knowing.

"It is the most impressive chamber within the castle. It is very well protected. It has always been the Lord of the castle's chamber. Merm will continue the tradition. It is the way. The chamber attracts those who lead a people. He will be there, I know." Darla couldn't properly explain why she was so certain of all this, but hoped Eruinn and Thiunn could accept this explanation for now. It was all tied into the Magic, Norkleau and the Old Ones.

"There is also other danger. With our awakening, there was bound to be an awakening of the *evil*. It will soon be able to detect our very presence and will no doubt, attempt to stop us by alerting Merm to our purpose."

"What is the *Evil*?" Thiunn wondered out loud.

"All the lust, greed and negative desires of the worlds focused together. I have never seen them, but was warned of their power by my mentors. Until they unlock the *Passwords* their magic is limited, after..." Darla never finished, leaving it to the imagination.

"Darla, Thiunn and I heard voices when we were under the water. I didn't mention it before, since I believed it was only happening to me and not of importance. Was it something else?"

"It was the voice of the Old Ones. They are here to help guide and encourage us. They are within each of us. They cannot physically intervene, only instruct and advise. Now that you are Chosen, they will make their thoughts more available to you when the need arises. Do not wait for their words. Continue to trust your own beings, but when they speak, listen.

Does everyone understand what we're doing?"

There were nods all the way round.

"Then Julian," Darla leaned towards him and gave a warm hug with a kiss, "we'll see you soon."

"Good luck," Julian whispered as she pulled back. With both hands upon the youngsters she led them off toward the passage to the castle room of Merm.

Not Long after their departure, a dark silence wrapped about Julian. He was totally immersed in blackness. Paranoia lurked at his every side.

A panic set in. Had they just left or was it long ago. Julian sought the beam from the peep hole using it as a mental reference. He was awake not asleep. This wasn't a dream.

He could picture his face and body in his mind though it was impossible to see. Were his eyes opened or closed? He took his fingers to discover the truth. He told himself to get a grip on himself.

"JULIAN."

He held his breath, taking his mind off the ring in his ears that grew with each moment of silence.

"Julian."

There it was again!

"Julian."

"Who's there! Wha...wha...What do you want?! Whe...wher...Where are you?!"

"Julian, it is me."

"Keep away from me!" the panic was immeasurable. Was this real or just his mind playing tricks.

"Julian."

A glowing came out of the dark from above. Closer it came. Julian backed away till he could go no further.

"Don't be afraid my son." A holographic image formed from within the glow. Was he dreaming! He began to shudder with cold apprehension.

"It is me, your father."

"Father?!" Julian's familiarity with the sound of the voice, slowly calmed him. He started to rise above the fear and ask more meaningful questions

"Father, is that really you?"

"Yes, boy. I'm here."

"Really, or is this a dream? Am I going mad?"

"No...you are not mad...I am here to help you. You must not tell the others that I came to you. What I have to speak of is only for the Stoneman's son. It is a part of our privilege for keeping the commitment. The commitment that has been passed on from son to son. The need has arrived. I am here to reveal the secrets that will be required to protect the Magic of the Old Ones that has been left in our trust."

"You mean the Key?"

"Yes and more. There is powerful magic that the Key can unlock. It must not be permitted. It will only corrupt and unleash *Evil* in the worlds. Misery and despair will live on forever. Only the Keepers of the Trust are immune to its lure. We are those Keepers."

"But why haven't you come before. All those times before?"

"The need is now. The *Evil* is awake and near. It is preparing to dominate the holder of the Key."

"But Merm has the Key. I don't see him giving in to anyone."

"It is out of his control. The *Evil* works with the greed, and corrupts the holder. We are the only ones who are incorruptible by the lure of its powerful magic. The *Evil* has no influence over us. We may use the Magic to protect and hide the Key from all others and thereby maintain the Balance in the worlds. It is our entrusted obligation. You must use the Key to re-establish the Balance, and then return it to a place of safety."

"How will I do all that?"

"You will know at the time. A place is being prepared."

"By whom and where? What about the Balance?"

"When the Key is in your control, call upon the Magic to stop the *Evil* that spreads. It will respond only when it is assured of your capacity as Keeper."

"How will it determine my capacity?"

"You will know at the time."

"At the time! I should know now! I should be prepared."

"You are prepared. We have all been prepared for generations. There is no more to say."

"Don't leave. A moment longer please."

The image began a gradual fade.

"Father....Father....I love you...! Father!"

Before total disappearance a smile filled his father's face. Julian could not keep himself from weeping from the emotional realization of all that had occurred. Had it been a dream? Or had his father really been there conversing as if nothing had ever changed in their lives? Julian would not torment himself. He accepted all that had gone by. It was real in his thoughts. That was all that mattered. He looked to the peep hole to confirm his wakefulness. The beam of light was still pouring through. He was reassured. How he had missed his father! It had been so hard growing up through those critical times, absent of a trusting male to give solace and support. He wondered at how he had managed to stumble to this age and seem so strong and aware to others, but not to himself. How he wished he could be sure that he was doing the right things; making the right choices. How he wished he had had more time to get the answers to all his childhood fears and doubts. They had never entirely left, but still held a grip on his soul. He was in the dark, but not alone.

- - - - - - - - - - - - - - - - - - -

Lenore was saying a prayer far in the South. She begged for the protection of the only two living statements of her married love. She prayed for Julian, her connection to her youth. She prayed for her mother who had died after giving birth to her brother; a mother she could barely remember, Lenore being an infant at the time. She prayed for the salvation of the worlds from the impending *Evil*. How she wished her father were still here. He would instill a sense of security and wellness. It wasn't easy being a mother alone. Sometimes she just wanted to be little again, without the cares and responsibilities of adulthood. To come and go, her main priority to dream of the future and imagine all the lovely possibilities. How different it had all been and now the gnawing fear of being left alone, again. She wasn't strong enough to start all over again. It wasn't right. It wasn't fair! "*PLEASE HELP US !*"

The tunnel did nothing but rise. Its walls suddenly changed from carved rock to slabs of granite. These were the castle foundations.

"Good, we are at the castle. Just a little further ahead should be stairs and torches that we can light using the flints that should also be near." The torches were made of easily flammable materials and they would certainly be able to set them alight without difficulty.

"This is quite some place. Who built all this?" Eruinn was looking ahead to where the stairs came into sight.

"Long ago after the Old Ones went on, their descendant worlds developed into highly skilled and artistic people. The group at Norkleau prided themselves in their architectural prowess. They built all this and attached it to the existing underground network. They always wanted alternate routes in times of threat, though they were mostly used as unnoticed passages for friends and lovers."

"Lovers? That sounds a bit far fetched."

"Not so far, Eruinn. They valued privacy and this was an excellent way to keep knowledge of their comings and goings less public."

"What romantic stories could be told." Thiunn the dreamer was captivated by the adventure of those rendezvous!

"Yes, maybe you could write one, after all this is over." Eruinn was pulling his leg.

"Come on you two, do not be so critical of each other. Who knows what you each are to accomplish? Bring the illuminator over here. I think this is it."

They walked on and were now at the base of the staircase. Eruinn shone the light near the right of the spiral metal stairs. There was a torch and flints beside it. Darla reached for the torch that was being held four lengths off the floor by a wall bracket.

"Thiunn, get the flints." Darla directed. Thiunn stepped over and grabbed two.

"Here you go."

"Thanks. Now in a moment..." she was hitting the two stones together, aiming the ensuing sparks in the direction of the dry torch. After several attempts one spark started to smolder. "Here we go. Blow on the sparks."

Both Thiunn and Darla blew. A small flame began. They had light.

"How long will it last?" asked Eruinn putting the illuminator into his pocket.

"Long enough for our purposes. Well..." She looked upward through the stairs, "...ready?"

Darla went first, Thiunn second, and Eruinn holding up the rear. Up they circled. It was a long flight. They had to stop twice to catch their breath and to prevent any dizziness from the spiral climb. They came to several landings with offshoots from the stairs. Darla kept climbing upward. Finally there was an end. There was a rickety metal platform with a handle built into the granite slab the stairs ended into. The slab was large enough to allow the entrance, or exit of a normal Southlander. There were four massive hinges and a latch. It would swing inward. They all stood still.

"What time will it be in there?"

"The middle of the night I hope. Merm, if he is here, should be asleep. The whole castle should be. We must be quiet. Eruinn you will stay here with the torch. Do not completely close the door after Thiunn and I enter the room. We won't be long. If anything goes wrong, I will yell out to shut the door. Do not re-open it, but go back to your Uncle. He will know what to do next."

"Don't let anything happen. Please be careful!"

"We will brother." Thiunn clasped his hand on Eruinn's right shoulder.

"Don't worry you two. I have Jewel to see us through. She hasn't let me down yet."

They all took a deep breath in preparation of the next incredible step.

"On the count of three we'll unlatch and open the slab. One...two...*THREE!*" Darla undid the latch.

The Lord had fallen into a fast, deep sleep, partially due to fatigue, but also Dorluc. He could now be greatly influenced.

Shortly after he had started to dream, Dorluc began his intervention. It was easier now that Merm wore the Key. The help of his subordinates had greatly increased the power of his magic far beyond the current drained levels.

Merm went through his usual recurrent visions of glory and success. He was riding a powerful horse leading thousands of his loyal Troops. There were cheers. He could see himself so pleased.

Then he was on a throne, with others paying homage, bowing, and gesticulating reverence. Dorluc's influence had begun. Slower and slower Merm's dream was being infiltrated. The images of success stronger and stronger—then a sense of loss. Something was wrong. He was falling, falling, fall.........ing. The Key! He felt for it around his neck. Its cold metallic touch reassured him. He needed the Key. He must use the Key to stop falling. Merm was tossing in his bed in the castle room. Then Dorluc spoke to him:

"I am the servant of the Key. You are my new master. Tell me your wishes."

Merm answered in his dream:

"The Magic and power of invincibility."

"It is as you wish. But beware. Beware strangers. They seek the Key. They wish to destroy you. They are here in the castle. You must find the real Magic. The *Passwords of Promise*. The Key will release their power. It must be done, or all will be lost."

Merm was accepting all that was said. He would discover the place of the *Passwords* and acquire their mysteries.

"Do not waste a moment. When the *Passwords* are yours, say this phrase:

'From all before is once more,
release upon me now.'

Do not forget!"

This sentence would really release Dorluc from his imprisonment, thereby enslaving Merm and all under his command. It had worked! Merm would now prioritize the finding of the hiding place of the *Passwords of Promise*.

Dorluc gradually removed his influence and pulled back to his own sphere. He would wait and watch until his moment of release arrived. Merm went back into a restful sleep.

Their timing and luck were incredible. Just as they opened the secret door, Dorluc had finished with his influence and had turned his attention elsewhere.

It was dark. Darla glanced through the compact opening. The room wasn't huge, but there was a large window to her left, a table in the center, and to her right a bed. Someone, she assumed Merm, though she had never seen him, was asleep. The room had light sandstone colored walls, no corners, rather curved meetings. It must be a tower turret room. There was light from a fireplace, which was now burning low. Other than the occasional crackle, everything was asleep.

Darla turned her head back toward Thiunn and in sign language explained their moves. They would start at the table and search, keeping a constant eye on the sleeping Lord. She crawled into the room, feeling exposed. Behind her and rising up to a door were stone stairs. The secret passage was under them. On tip toes she went to the table.

Thiunn was just as cautious as he entered the room of his enemy. He also took a good view about the room, being awed and fearful. Out he stepped, following Darla.

The table was a mess and came up to Darla's shoulder. They would have to climb upon the chairs for a look. Paper and more paper, books and pens, spilt ink. Darla put one page in her pocket, without a word. Thiunn rifled through and felt his fingers hit a small box like object. He motioned to Darla to check his find.

It was a box, about the size of the impression from the safe in the Lost Palace below, that she and Julian had examined earlier. Thiunn was motioned by her to pick it up and pass it to her. She took hold of it and while taking a breath, carefully opened...it sounded its short tune!...Inside there was nothing but a space where a key must have been. Her heart dropped.

The sleeping body of the Lord Merm tossed to one side. His face was looking in their direction. He was asleep. A glitter was given off by the gold chain round his neck. Darla instantly knew where to find the Key. She pointed so Thiunn would understand. The Key was not in the box but was on his necklace! They would have to get it!

- - - - - - - - - - - - - - - - - -

Dorluc was feeling troubled. He didn't know why, but decided to check on Merm. As he looked into his viewer, he saw what was about to happen to the Key!

"Stop!" he cried, of course no one could hear. He must get back into Merm's dreams and rouse him, in order to stop these two! He called out for his others to help.

- - - - - - - - - - - - - - - - - -

Across the room in front of the huge figure. Thiunn and Darla stood nervously. There was no time to spare.

Darla decided to lift the chain till the Key was visible. Thiunn would find and undo the clasp, while Darla fed the chain through the hole in the Key. They must HURRY!

Dorluc was busy focusing his magic and gradually invading Merm's dreams once more. It was taking so long.

A gentle click, Merm moved. They both thought that was it, but he settled. Darla fed the chain.

Merm was seeing danger in his dreams, but Dorluc hadn't been able to awaken him yet. A few more thoughts...

She had it! Thiunn turned. Merm was going to wake! He indicated this to Darla. They both ran for the secret door.

Dorluc was warning Merm:

"Wake up. They steal the Key. Wake up!"

Thiunn was first to pass through the secret entrance, and was waiting and ready to close the door after Darla passed through.

Just as Darla was to enter, she dropped the Key. That noise, along with Dorluc's warning, awoke the Lord. She groped on the dark floor looking for the Key.

"Hey! You there! Guards! GUARDS!" Merm was up and out of bed on his way to Darla.

"Darla hurry!" Thiunn had visions of another capture.

"I can't see it! Yes. There it is! Don't wait. Go on without me!" Darla picked up the Key from the floor in front of her. Not sure of what to do next. She became desperate.

"No! Hurry! We can wait!" Thiunn though scared, could wait. He did not want things to end this way!

"Stop!" yelled Merm. During the few instants of all the commotion, Merm had now totally reawakened. He could clearly see the secret entrance and Darla. He must catch this thief!

Dorluc was watching through his view screen, trapped within his formless world. He was on edge with apprehension, watching on helplessly as he saw his own chances of escape, escaping!

Chapter 13.

All of Mal's Guard units crept to their positions. Their first task was to disable the watch, then while the Gott Troopers slept, remove as many of the weapons as they could. It would be a tent by tent effort. One by one the Guard progressed.

The Gotts were in the habit of leaving their weapons by the inside of the main front flap. The tents were easy to enter and the Guard managed to squeeze into and remove all the arms that they could find. Each Guard member, acted as a part of a human chain removing the weapons. Once they had secured a large number of arms, placing them just outside the perimeter, they were now ready to begin phase two of their plan. Meanwhile Mal, having waited till he felt the first phase was complete, began with his own unit, the assault on the tavern headquarters. Mal believed that the capture of any Gott commanders would hasten any routing. Timing and a great deal of luck would determine the final outcome!

Through the trees and down the incline Mal and his unit traversed. The other units must have accomplished their goals by this point. Not a single sentry was in sight. Mal's unit was within twenty lengths of the tavern and had fanned out to surround the edifice. He motioned all to crouch and await the start of phase two.

Phase two would bring a sudden noise of attack. Every Trooper in the encampment would be startled and confused. Unable to find their weapons they would panic. That was the hope. The remaining Troopers in the tavern would then exit to see what was happening.

Mal's unit would pick them off as they ran out, then storm the tavern, taking care not to harm any Gotts who might be of command rank. It sounded straight forward. The first battle cry rang out. There was no turning back!

The Units that were besieging the encamped Troops, were coming in from three sides. This left only one possible escape route for the Troopers. They would be forced back through the fields to the North from which they had come. There was mayhem. The noise of the attacking Jard Guard was deafening. For the Gott caught unaware, it appeared as if a tremendous force had set in upon them from nowhere. Everything was happening so fast!

By reflex the Gott Troops awoke to the ensuing alarm. Quickly they pulled on boots and grabbed whatever clothing that could rapidly be put on. They were startled and disoriented, a disorientation that led to panic when they were unable to find their weapons! One by one each Trooper searched, trying to determine if it was his weapon alone that was misplaced, or something far worse! Once the realization of their attack by the Guard, and then lack of munitions had set in, the Troopers began to pull back, back to the only apparent safe avenue—northward.

What was going on? They had been assured by Command that the Jard Guard was weak and small in number, being unable to respond. Now here they were vastly outnumbering them!

The Jard Guard had always been a respected fighting force by their enemies. They were well known for their ferocity and determination. The Separation War gave many examples of their professionalism in battle. Most Gott Troopers had heard and a few had experienced first hand, the legendary skill of the Guard, with its invincibility and magic-like strength. They had no desire to confront them, especially without weapons.

Their Captains yelled orders as the main Gott force panicked. They were to regroup northward. An even more disorganized scene developed. The surprise attack by the Guard was working. It was too soon even for the Guard to realize this success or to ponder the next question of how long the victory could be maintained? Thank goodness all, including the confusion which the early darkness had contributed, had linked together to create the desired effects. But once the light was strong enough this might change. The Gott Troops would then realize that they had been fooled. It wouldn't take them long to use what weapons they could muster to counter the attack.

At the sound of the early disorder at the Gott headquarters, the tavern lights had come on and Troopers began to come out into the still dark morning. They weren't many in number. This was encouraging. Mal's unit went into action. The Troopers were disabled. After the exterior had been secured, Mal took his remaining force and broke through the tavern door.

It was dim and once inside, each of Mal's unit hugged the protection of walls, chairs and dividers. They cleared the way for a thorough and safe capture of any Gotts within the tavern headquarters. With all the confusion of the surprise attack, the few Troopers found inside, were startled and not sure of what was happening.

Mal directed his unit: "Take them." he was indicating the Troopers. Then…"Three of you,…go upstairs into the rooms! See who else is here and seize them!"

There were no niceties in action. It was a matter of the bare necessities of communication to achieve the objectives as safely and efficiently as could be. Everyone understood perfectly. While the Unit secured the lower level, three Guards went upstairs and found a Trooper of rank. They shouted down to Mal:

"Sir! We have one!" and there being pushed ahead of them to the balustrade, which overlooked the main tavern, they presented Frid.

"One has escaped out the window just as we broke into their room. We got this one. He was stuck half way through. Fat isn't he!" They continued pushing him on and down the stairs.

"Who are you! By what right..." he was complaining all the way. Down the stairs he continued into the main dinning room where he was pushed in front of Mal.

"Exactly. Perhaps you could explain this Gott presence hereabouts?" Mal was defiant.

"To whom do I address myself!" Frid played his expected role.

"Area Chief Mal, Jard Guard. Sir, you are my prisoner."

"Frid, Commander, Seventh Division. That is all I will say."

"Well, Frid, Commander. If you want to see your homeland again, you had better prove that there is some value to keeping you alive!"

"That is against the Treaty!" there was now a nervousness to Blag's tone.

"Treaty? Don't talk to me of Treaty! With your present violations, I'd say your lucky we have even bothered to stop to ask questions before we kill! Now, what are you here for and who are you?!"

Frid, though captured by the enemy, managed to remain confident in his, and the Gott ability to turn this situation around and to prevail once again. He would tell this Mal a half truth and that was all.

"We are reclaiming that which was wrongfully taken from the Gotts! Enjoy yourself while you can. There are many more of us nearby. When you are my prisoner we will discover your own fiber, strand by strand!" Frid spat on Mal. It was to be expected.

"Chain him to a pole outside. We will see how long it will take this barking dog to change to whimpers."

Frid was carted out to the front of the tavern. Mal was pleased. Everything had so far worked nicely. It was funny how things either succeeded or failed so swiftly. But then he realized from all his experience that this was usually the case!

As the new light of the morning cascaded through the trees the satisfaction of victory, no matter how transitory, tasted sweet. All the Units of the Guard had performed their jobs well. The Gott Troopers had been routed.

After the perimeter had been secured, each of the unit captains were to come to the tavern for debriefing by Mal. Eventually all arrived to find the tavern under the control of the Guard and a joyous Colleg thanking Mal for his deliverance.

"Oh, thank the stars you came. I thought all was lost. You obviously got my message?"

"So the bird was from you? Yes, your alert was well timed, but I don't know how long this liberation will hold. We are limited in number here. It will still require some effort to bring up the main force. We may not be able to hold on that long," Mal was cautioning Colleg.

Colleg was unimpressed. He only cared that he was free of the Gotts. Worry about tomorrow, tomorrow!

"Tell me what you know of all this." Mal opened his hands outward to indicate the surrounding area.

"Very little, 'cept it all started with a wounded female one, two or so nights ago. She was on the run."

"A female? Who? Can you describe her?" Mal was interested. Could it be connected to the recent trouble that Zer had told him about in Jard?

"A magnificent creature. Proud, silky hair."

"Ah...please continue the story. How did you know she was on the run?"

"Wounded, alone, no bag, not of these parts. On top of that, a Trooper and a Horseman came asking about her not long after she left. She ate quickly and then continued on her journey. I invited her to stay the night, as she was obviously exhausted, but her determination or fright propelled her on. Looking back, I see she was trying to keep ahead of those two." He meant the Gott Commanders who had first taken his tavern, of whom Mal's unit had captured one.

"For what reason?"

"No idea. She didn't talk much."

"Then what?"

"Next I know, this fat Frid, and his second Tosh..." Mal connected this 'Tosh' to be the escapee Gott Commander from the room upstairs, "...were taking over my tavern for a headquarters, and telling me that their conquest had begun! I was only kept alive while I was of value! Somehow I got the message off and just prayed it would be delivered. Presto, you are here and I'm free. Thank you. Thank you all!" he started his non stop chatter of praise.

"Colleg. Please. My unit has thirst, could you?"

"Say no more Captain. The very least I can do. On the house!" Colleg, pleased to be able to return a favor, rushed to the kitchen. His leaving had served two purposes. One, privacy for Mal to debrief and two, an end to his chatter.

Once Colleg had left, Mal turned to the members of his unit who had been reporting to the tavern and congratulated them:

"It has worked. I congratulate you all. Sit." Seeing that most of his captains were now present, Mal began the meeting. They were in the center of the room using the largest table.

"We will have to plan well our immediate future. By evening a counter attack will materialize. We have captured a Gott Commander, which might slow them a little, but I doubt it."

"Was that who the creature was outside! I threw a rock at him, to try and shut him up. It hit his head, having no effect." joked one of his captains.

They were all in good spirits and continued to joke for a bit, then proceeded to get down to the next business: surviving till reinforcements arrived!

Earlier Tosh, upon hearing the noise of the attack, had jumped to the window of the second floor room. He and Frid were having a short conference. They had been up all night and were about to retire. Seeing Mal's unit, he quickly decided to exit via the window as the Jardians entered the tavern. Frid was to follow. He quickly pulled himself through the small window. Upon landing on the hard ground he saw Frid being pulled back into the room. A Guard looked out and saw him below. He was spotted. Tosh ran straight to the northern path, being rapidly absorbed and hidden by the trees and shrubs. The only thought that crossed his mind at the time was that he had been lucky. He must find the rear Troop Division. News of the Jard Guard, and the attack must be relayed to the Lord. Frid's fate was his own. The fat old fool!

Chapter 14.

Eruinn was alarmed. He was still in the passage and couldn't see what was happening, "Thiunn what's going on!"

"It's Darla! I think Merm has caught hold of her, and is pulling her back! Grab my belt and pull! I've got her hands!"

Darla, realizing the situation, encouraged Thiunn to let go, "Take the Key. TAKE the Key! It will be our only chance!"

"No. We can get you in!" Thiunn did not want to give up.

The tugging was stalemated. Merm now had a strong grip.

"Take the Key!" Darla wasn't asking.

"Darla I won't leave you." Thiunn was almost apologizing.

Again everything was occurring so fast. Two Troopers were answering their Lord's call. It would be moments and then they would be helping him. The stalemate would be easily broken.

"Take the Key and leave me. I'll be all right. Get to Julian fast. He will be able to use the Magic to help,"

She began to transfer the Key to Thiunn through one of her clasped hands. Thiunn had it now in his grasp. With a parting look their eyes met. She smiled, winked and released her grip upon Thiunn. Thiunn could not hold her alone. Thiunn and Eruinn fell back into the passage after the suddenness of Darla's letting go. The secret door slammed shut. Darla was gone and they were alone!

"Thiunn? Darla?" Eruinn was almost in tears.

"We have only one choice left to us: Uncle Julian must get the Key, so that he can help Darla," Thíunn's apprehension was strong, "I can't bear the thought of Darla captured by Merm. He will certainly torture her."

"Maybe not. He will want the Key back. Darla has value as a hostage. Thiunn, it won't take those Troopers long to break down the secret door. We must get as far ahead as we can now!"

"You're right. Let's get back to Uncle Julian."

Thiunn placed the Key in his pocket. Eruinn picked up the still lit torch. They were off on their return. Thiunn had not noticed, in the urgency, that the Key was becoming warmer. Merm's placing it upon the necklace, was igniting its magical power. The two Chosen Ones would have to place it into the safety of the hands of Julian before even they were affected by its corrupting powers. Then the destiny of the Stoneman's son would begin to be fulfilled. From all the ages before, the promise would be kept, he was the Keeper!

As they hurriedly descended the stairs of their return journey, the noise of picks against the solid passage door became loudly audible. They prayed as they went that Julian would be reached in time to do whatever he was able, once the Key was in his care.

"Gotcha you little thief! You Troopers go and get picks and bring back a crew. We will break down this escape route and follow whoever else is in there."

"Yes Lord."

They left. One sole Trooper remained holding on to Darla with her arms twisted behind her back.

"Your gonna twist my arm off if you keep that up!" complained Darla.

"So you must be the female that escaped from the Keep. That is quite an historic precedent. So, you came for the Key? Give it!" Merm was under the impression that Darla still had the Key and that it had not been stolen completely from him.

"What Key?" Darla played dumb.

"You know what I mean. Search her."

The Trooper began searching the struggling female. In the process he ripped and tore her clothing. Darla tried to conceal her partial uncovering. She was offended more than frightened.

"Take your dirty paws off!"

"Lord, a sword!" The Trooper offered it to Merm.

"Ah, the magic weapon we have heard of. Let's see it closer."

He took the Jewel and began to examine it. Darla, seeing the opportunity, sang out a short melody. The sword flashed out light from the precious stones on its hilt. They were blinding. In the blinding flash of the lights, Darla was let go by the Trooper. Jewel became hot in the grip of Merm. It was so hot that it burnt his hand. Merm let out a cry of pain and let go of the sword. Instantly Jewel flew into Darla's waiting hand. Darla would make her stand.

Just as all this was happening the other Troopers returned with picks in hand, they struck from behind. Then, with the heavy handle of one tool Darla was hit on the head. She fell to the floor unconscious. The sword dimmed once again. It lay by her side, still in the grip of her left hand.

"She has a lot of spunk this female. Take her and tie her. We will bring her with us, and find the thieves."

"Lord why not kill her now?"

"She will be of more use to use alive. Maybe her friends will want her and be willing to trade for her life. They have something that I want returned."

"Lord?" asked another Trooper, "Where are we to dig?"

"Not dig! Break those stones in the wall down, and hurry!" Merm indicated where the entrance had been. His hand hurt and his mood reflected his discomfort.

The Troopers complied and started slamming away

at the place in the wall where Merm had seen the other intruder vanish. The bits of stone shattered and sprayed throughout the room.

Merm was unhappy. The warning in the dream had been too late. He was being driven to recapture the Key, but who was directing? He couldn't stop to consider now. He must pick up the chase, before they got too far a lead.

As the Troopers swung their picks, Dorluc was once again trying to reach Merm. He whispered in Merm's subconscious.

"The Lost Palace. They will go to the Palace. They seek another. The Stoneman. Their flight will begin from there. Go. Go!"

Merm abruptly changed his mind. "You keep digging. When you are through, follow after the best you can. I want that thief alive! You three bring the female and come with me. You! Tell Rmont to meet me in the Lost Palace. *MOVE!*"

Darla, still knocked out, was lifted to the back of a Trooper. Merm carefully considered what he would do about her sword. He wanted this sword and would learn how to control its magic. He prodded it once, then twice with a finger, testing its condition. After realizing that Jewel was no longer a threat, but still nursing his burnt hand, he ordered one of the Troopers to pick it up and follow to the rear as he turned to go up the stairs and on to the Lost Palace.

Merm and Dorluc grieved for the loss of the Key!

Eruinn lead the way hoping not to make any mistakes. They didn't have any time to lose. Thiunn's mind was on Darla. He prayed for her safety. They found themselves back upon the path to the Lost Palace. Without warning, the voice from the underwater passage spoke.

"Chosen One, the path is straight, do not fall. The Keeper knows the way to end all." it repeated in the stillness of the tunnel.

"Eruinn. Did you just hear a voice? It was the same one of the water passage."

"Yeah. Speaking in a riddle?"

"Yeah." They discussed the words and their meaning.

"After we deliver the Key it will be up to us to find Darla. We can't abandon her to these Gotts."

"I know. After all she took care of me at the Lake. I owe her a big one."

On they went.

Julian, still sitting in the dark, knew what he was meant to do. When the Key was given, he must go and sing the tune of old in front of the safe, while holding the Key in his left hand. Another door would open, revealing the *Passwords* in two small leather bound books. He was to remove them and placing the Key in between the two, sing the four note melody and say:

> *"Undo all evil magic,*
> *Give back peaceful home,*
> *Safe return the Chosen,*
> *Balance out this storm."*

It didn't make alot of sense. He just knew he had to chant it. He just knew! This was all part of the deeply buried mysteries kept within him. It would then be his job to hide the Key far from here, in the secret place of the Old. He knew where to go. All he awaited now was his three companions with the Key.

He was subdued and resolved to the responsibility ahead. Everything was becoming perfectly clear. He wondered though, if he would remember after he had completed the task, or find himself again the host to a dormant soul. As he postulated an answer, Eruinn and Thiunn nosily came into earshot.

"Uncle J!" Thiunn called out first.

Julian looked in the direction of the sound and shortly a torch light became visible. He strained to see that all was well. One, two,... there were only two!

"Who's there?"

"Eruinn, and I. Darla has been captured, but we bring the Key. Darla told us to hurry. The Gotts will soon be upon us all."

There wasn't time to explain, but all understood.

The picks broke through the stone swiftly. After a little widening to accommodate their enormity, three Troopers entered and with bright light sticks started the chase.

Lord Merm had also made good speed. He was almost at the opening of the excavation to the Lost Palace. Rmont, Citol, and another were awaiting his arrival in front of the rock door. He greeted the surprised threesome with the appearance of the recaptured female.

"I see you recognize her. We will keep her with us. When she comes to, there are questions to extricate answers, willingly or not."

He took Rmont to one side: "They have taken the Key. I think they are coming here. We have to beat them!"

All ran past the rock door into the tunnel. They would be in front of the safe where the Key had been discovered within moments.

Thiunn leaped towards Julian.

"Here's the Key. Please hurry. Darla's life might be at stake, as well as many others in the worlds!"

"Don't worry little one." Julian's voice was stranger than normal. "All will be fine. I know what to do. Follow me. Do not let me be prevented from my path."

They went up again to the secret door that entered into the Lost Palace where they had taken the Gott stew and carefully opened it. The two youngsters were feeling something powerful begin to swell within them. After the entrance was opened and it was clear that they were safe, Julian crept out and crossing the short distance, stopped in front of the tiny wall safe that had held the Key. He then sang the tune of the Keepers.

Just as Julian began the tune, Merm entered the area and saw the Jardian semi concealed under the grand statues and in front of the wall safe. He called out to his Troopers to:

"STOP THEM!"

They were discovered and twenty Troopers were headed their way.

Eruinn and Thiunn turned to face the onslaught. They would try to allow their uncle to continue his task undisturbed. They each took a few steps towards the Troopers into clear view and then knelt down. Without their awareness they resembled the two stone statues to their sides above. They went into a deep trance. They were transferring their consciousness out of themselves, but to where was it going and to what purpose?!

Julian sang again. There was a shudder throughout the ground and another door within the safe opened. He saw the *Passwords*. The Books were bound in beautiful red leather. Julian threw his free hand out and grabbed them.

The two youngsters were now completely entranced. The opening of the inner safe had hastened their transference. The two large stone statues of the seated men trembled more and more. Merm and his Troopers were almost upon them.

Julian grabbed the *Passwords*, placed the Key in between, and said:

> *"Undo all evil magic,*
> *Give back peaceful home,*
> *Safe return the Chosen,*

Balance out this storm."

Upon the utterance of each word there exploded a vast lighted ball out of nowhere. Looking up it could be seen that the shudder on the ground was being caused by the statues. The statues of stone were coming alive! They were acting upon the will of Eruinn and Thiunn. As the statues shook, it became clear that they were about to rise from their seats and step down to confront the Gott Troops! Slowly they rose and began to step down looking in the Gotts' direction. This halted Lord Merm in his steps towards the thieves. It was a terrifying experience to behold. The huge inanimate stone statues were living! They would battle the Gott Troopers below! The room was filled with screams of terror and rumbling rock.

As all this proceeded, Darla, who was with Merm and still being held captive upon the back of a Trooper, awoke to the whinnying of Jewel. The sword was being affected by the magic of the Key and *Passwords of Promise*. It was beginning to glow and awaken without the help of Darla. There was a greater force at work now! Jewel managed, in the chaos, to free itself of the grip of the one Trooper and fly free, impaling the other who was carrying Darla. The Trooper fell to the ground. Darla struggled free, pulled her weapon out of his body and ran to the aid of her compatriots.

"Julian, into the passage!" She was waving Jewel at the startled Gotts and running to him. The whole cavern was shaking and about to crumble. She must get Eruinn and Thiunn into the passageway after Julian.

Slapping them, she tried to awake them. Nothing happened. The cavern was about to crumble. She took the hilt of her sword, placed the jewels on their forehead, and sang the four notes of old. They started to wake from their trance.

"Come on, let's go! Into the passageway." She tugged at them.

They began to realize the impending doom of the

cavern. They each dragged themselves, with Darla's help, out of the cavern and into the passageway. Bang, the door closed. Just then the roof caved in.

"What was that!" Thiunn, not fully recovered asked.

"Your Uncle J's singing brought the house down!" Darla joked.

"What about Merm and his Troopers?" Eruinn asked.

"I didn't see. I hope they were trapped under all that."

They sat for a moment to catch their breath the torch light dim. When they were over their shock, Darla began a mental check of the party. Eruinn Thiunn...

"Julian? Julian...JULIAN!" her voice became loud.

" Julian,...where are you!" They all became alarmed. Where had he gone?

"Darla, we can't remain here long. Troopers are past the castle's secret door. Eruinn and I heard them breaking through. Julian must have gone on ahead. We'll catch up."

"It's odd of him to go off like that though." said a worried Darla.

"He'll be fine. We've come through all this! What could be worse?" Thiunn's point made sense. They would move on in hope of finding Julian at the Lake of Choices.

News of the cave-in spread throughout Norkleau. Crews were enlisted to dig for survivors. No one was certain of the condition or whereabouts of their Lord. The slave labor feverishly dug.

At the same time of all this activity, the Jard Guard was planning its strategy for the next phase of their victory. Colleg was serving them drinks. Just before the cave in at Norkleau and after the words of Julian had been expressed, a tremor shook the ground in the North. It was disconcerting to all. Especially the routed Gott Troops who were now totally enervated. Too many unexpected things were going on.

Tosh had made it back to the bulk of the routed Troops to the North. It wasn't a nice scene, nothing but confusion. Most of the force, after the earth tremors, were only interested in continuing their retreat. There was no organized leadership to bridle the panic. He must try to regain command in order to prevent a total disaster.

Finding a higher spot he began shouting out for the Troopers to stop. It was a foolish effort. He continued, knowing from his vast experience in the field, that the situation could still be turned around. If only he could get enough of them to listen, the rest would look after itself! But it was already too late.

In all the places throughout the worlds, at the time after Julian's disappearance from Darla, Eruinn and Thiunn, came a God-like voice and image. Its timing was superb. It followed the tremendous shake that rumbled the ground. This added to the fear and bewilderment of the disoriented Gott Troopers.

You will Stop!

The Balance is restored.

The tremors began again, but this time, only in the area of the *Evil's* agents, who still were attempting to get away from whoever or whatever was going on.

Return, or be destroyed!

Again, the voice spoke a message that was directed against the *evil* of the Gotts.

We are the Old,

and our Magic strong!

Begone disturbers of peace!

So much had occurred in the past few days. It had ended as fast as it had begun! After the tremors and the warning of the voices, the Gott Troops had definitely given up any thought of regrouping. Tosh's effort, was now useless. The Division would continue their run to the North. Back to what they believed would be the safety of home. They would be pursued by the Guard. This thought, along with the voicings, completed the quashing of the invasion. It was now the job of the Jard Guard to clean up any stragglers! The Gotts scrambled to retreat. When the clean up was finished, the authorities would have to reevaluate the Treaty with the Gotts. The days of isolationism were no longer possible. They would have to deal harshly with the North once it could be established who was in charge!

Darla, Eruinn and Thiunn were well on their way to the secret entrance at the Lake of Choices. They each felt that Julian had gone on ahead and that they would meet him there. The three were not aware of all that had transpired between the Jard Guard and the Gott Seventh Division. They would find out in time. For now they were under the impression that a threat still existed and it did, but they were not aware of its scope! They could hardly wait to rejoin with Julian and determine their course of action. They each prayed that he was all right.

Something continued to gnaw away inside them throughout their journey. It was difficult to explain. They retraced the passage way without rest until they arrived at the Lake. After a short time of careful examination they realized that there was no sign of Julian. He hadn't come this way!

"What do we do now?" a concerned nephew uttered the words that they all were thinking.

The Gott conquest of the Southland had for the moment, been thwarted. It was not yet over. The Lord Merm had been found alive amongst the rubble of the cave-in and saved!

Lord Merm would continue, being guided through his subconscious awareness by Dorluc, the search for the thieves who had caused all the complications. It would never stop! The *Evil* would mercilessly hunt down every lead to locate them. Merm and Dorluc would be on their heels till the Key and *Passwords of Promise* were finally under their control. The thieves' flight would be arduous, both physically and spiritually. The adventure was really about to begin!

*   *   *   *

Far away to the northwest, in the middle of the Burning Forest, through the shadowy light of dusk, walked a determined sole figure.

It carried two red books and the Key.

*   *   *   *

About the Author

Terence Munsey lives in Richmond Hill, Ontario. He attended York University for undergraduate studies and then Stanford University for graduate studies, where he received an M.A. degree.

He has written four books in *The Stoneman Series:*

1. THE FLIGHT OF THE STONEMAN'S SON
2. THE KEEPER OF THREE
3. LABYRINTHS OF LIGHT
4. MARKS OF STONE

He loves to hear from his readers. Send or fax him a letter.

*Send $2.00 today and get your *official* 2&1/4in **STONEMAN SERIES** button.